MASTERPIECES OF
MYSTERY & DETECTION

Compiled by Rosamund Morris

HART PUBLISHING COMPANY, INC.

New York City, New York

ACKNOWLEDGMENTS

Grateful acknowledgment is made to the copyright owners for permission to reprint the following stories:

"The Inspiration of Mr. Budd" from *Sayers Holiday Book* by Dorothy L. Sayers, copyright 1939 by Dorothy Leigh Sayers Fleming; reprinted by kind permission of Harper & Row, Publishers, and David Higham Associates Ltd.

"The Problem of Cell 13" by Jacques Futrelle, copyright 1905, and re-registered 1933 by May Futrelle, Member Authors' League of America; reprinted by kind permission of Mrs. Jacques Futrelle.

"Shadowed by Death" from *The Confessions of Arsene Lupin* by Maurice Leblanc, copyright 1913 by Alexander Texira de Mattos; reprinted by kind permission of Claude Leblanc.

"The Invisible Man" from *The Innocence of Father Brown* by G. K. Chesterton; copyright 1911 by Dodd, Mead & Company; reprinted by kind permission of Dodd, Mead & Company, Inc., Miss D. E. Collins, and Messrs. Cassell & Co. Ltd.

"The Homesick Buick" by John D. MacDonald, copyright 1950 by John D. MacDonald; reprinted by kind permission of Littauer and Wilkinson.

"The Ace of Trouble" by C. Hedley Barker, copyright 1925 by C. Hedley Barker; reprinted by kind permission of John Farquharson Ltd., of London, England.

"The Five Orange Pips" from *The Adventures of Sherlock Holmes* by Sir Arthur Conan Doyle; reprinted by kind permission of the Trustees of the Estate of Sir Arthur Conan Doyle and John Murray Ltd.

"The Red-Headed League" from *The Adventures of Sherlock Holmes* by Sir Arthur Conan Doyle; reprinted by kind permission of the Trustees of the Estate of Sir Arthur Conan Doyle and John Murray Ltd.

"A Scandal in Bohemia" from *The Adventures of Sherlock Holmes* by Sir Arthur Conan Doyle; reprinted by kind permission of the Trustees of the Estate of Sir Arthur Conan Doyle and John Murray Ltd.

CONTENTS

DOROTHY LEIGH SAYERS
(1893-   )

... is one of the most influential detective writers of
this century. She has done much to change the face
of this particular genre. She is foremost among those
who have infused the traditional detective tale with
a literary style and deeply realized characters. In
"Murder Must Advertise," for example, Lord Peter
Wimsey, Dorothy Sayers' roguish detective-hero,
manages to direct some telling satire at the advertising business as he solves his murder. In "Gaudy
Night," both a mystery and a highly complex love
relationship are resolved.

"The Inspiration of Mr. Budd" represents Dorothy
Sayers in one of her more light-hearted moods.
This amiable story of a timid London hairdresser's
involvement in a murder is a deft blend of suspense
and humor.

THE INSPIRATION
OF MR. BUDD

leads to the capture of a dangerous criminal

£500 REWARD

The Evening Messenger, *ever anxious to further the ends of justice, has decided to offer the above reward to any person who shall give information leading to the arrest of the man, William Strickland, alias Bolton, who is wanted by the police in connection with the murder of the late Emma Strickland at 59 Acacia Crescent, Manchester.*

DESCRIPTION OF THE WANTED MAN

The following is the official description of William

Strickland: Age 43; height 6 ft. 1 or 2; complexion rather dark; hair silver-gray and abundant, may dye same; full gray mustache and beard, may now be clean-shaven; eyes light gray, rather close-set; hawk nose; teeth strong and white, displays them somewhat prominently when laughing, left upper eye-tooth stopped with gold; left thumb-nail disfigured by a recent blow.

Speaks in rather loud voice; quick, decisive manner. Good address.

May be dressed in a gray or dark blue lounge suit, with stand-up collar (size 15) and soft felt hat.

Absconded 5th inst., and may have left, or will endeavor to leave, the country.

MR. BUDD read the description through carefully once again and sighed. It was in the highest degree unlikely that William Strickland should choose his small and unsuccessful saloon, out of all the barbers' shops in London, for a haircut or a shave, still less for "dyeing same"; even if he was in London, which Mr. Budd saw no reason to suppose.

Three weeks had gone by since the murder, and the odds were a hundred to one that William Strickland had already left a country too eager with its offer of free hospitality. Nevertheless, Mr. Budd committed the description, as well as he could, to memory. It was a chance—just as the Great Crossword Tournament had been a chance, just as the Ninth Rainbow Ballot had been a chance, and the Bunko Poster Ballot, and the Monster Treasure Hunt organized by the *Evening Clarion*. Any headline with money in it could attract Mr. Budd's fascinated eye in these lean days, whether it offered a choice between fifty thousand pounds down and ten pounds a week for life, or merely a modest hundred or so.

It may seem strange, in an age of shingling and bingling, Mr. Budd should look enviously at Complete Lists of Prizewinners. Had not the hairdresser across the way, who only last year had eked out his mean ninepences with the yet meaner profits on cheap cigarettes and comic papers, lately bought out the greengrocer next door, and engaged a staff of exquisitely coiffed assistants to adorn his new "Ladies' Hairdressing Department" with its purple and orange curtains, its two rows of gleaming marble basins, and an apparatus like a Victorian chandelier for permanent waving?

Had he not installed a large electric sign surrounded by a scarlet border that ran round and round perpetually, like a kitten chasing its own tail? Was it not his sandwich-man even now patrolling the pavement with a luminous announcement of Treatment and Prices? And was there not at this moment an endless stream of young ladies hastening into those heavily-perfumed parlors in the desperate hope of somehow getting a shampoo and a wave "squeezed in" before closing-time?

If the reception clerk shook a regretful head, they did not think of crossing the road to Mr. Budd's dimly-lighted window. They made an appointment for days ahead and waited patiently, anxiously fingering the bristly growth at the back of the neck and the straggly bits behind the ears that so soon got out of hand.

Day after day Mr. Budd watched them flit in and out of the rival establishment, willing, praying even, in a vague, ill-directed manner, that some of them would come over to him; but they never did.

And yet Mr. Budd knew himself to be the finer artist. He had seen shingles turned out from over the way that he would never have countenanced, let alone charged three shillings and sixpence for. Shingles with an ugly hard line at the nape, shingles which were a slander on the shape of a good head or brutally emphasized the weak points of an ugly one; hurried, conscienceless shingles, botched work, handed over on a crowded afternoon to a girl who had only served a three years' apprenticeship and to whom the final mysteries of "tapering" were a sealed book.

And then there was the "tinting"—his own pet subject, which he had studied *con amore*—if only those too-sprightly matrons would come to him! He would gently dissuade them from that dreadful mahogany dye that made them look like metallic robots—he would warn them against that widely advertised preparation which was so incalculable in its effects; he would use the cunning skill which long experience had matured in him—tint them with the infinitely delicate art which conceals itself.

Yet nobody came to Mr. Budd but the navvies and the young loungers and the men who plied their trade beneath the naphtha-flares in Wilton Street.

And why could not Mr. Budd also have burst out into marble and electricity and swum to fortune on the rising tide?

The reason is very distressing, and, as it fortunately has no bearing on the story, shall be told with merciful brevity.

Mr. Budd had a younger brother, Richard, whom he had promised his mother to look after. In happier days Mr. Budd had owned a flourishing business in their native town of Northampton, and Richard had been a bank clerk. Richard had got into bad ways (poor Mr. Budd blamed himself dreadfully for this). There had been a sad affair with a girl, and a horrid series of affairs with bookmakers, and then Richard had tried to mend bad with worse by taking money from the bank. You need to be very much more skillful than Richard to juggle successfully with bank ledgers.

The bank manager was a hard man of the old school: he prosecuted. Mr. Budd paid the bank and the bookmakers, and saw the girl through her trouble while Richard was in prison, and paid for their fares to Australia when he came out, and gave them something to start life on.

But it took all the profits of the hairdressing business, and he couldn't face all the people in Northampton any more, who had known him all his life. So he had run to vast London, the refuge of all who shrink from the eyes of their neighbors, and bought this little shop in Pimlico, which had done fairly well, until the new fashion which did so much for other hairdressing businesses killed it for lack of capital.

That is why Mr. Budd's eye was so painfully fascinated by headlines with money in them.

He put the newspaper down, and as he did so, caught sight of his own reflection in the glass and smiled, for he was not without a sense of humor. He did not look quite the man to catch a brutal murderer single-handed. He was well on in the middle forties— a trifle paunchy, with fluffy pale hair, getting a trifle thin on top (partly hereditary, partly worry, that was), five feet six at most, and soft-handed, as a hairdresser must be.

Even razor in hand, he would hardly be a match for William Strickland, height six feet one or two, who had so ferociously battered his old aunt to death, so butcherly hacked her limb from limb, so horribly disposed of her remains in the copper. Shaking his head dubiously, Mr. Budd advanced to the door, to cast a forlorn eye at the busy establishment over the way, and nearly ran into a bulky customer who dived in rather precipitately.

"I beg your pardon, sir," murmured Mr. Budd, fearful of alienating ninepence; "just stepping out for a breath of fresh air, sir. Shave, sir?"

The large man tore off his overcoat without waiting for Mr. Budd's obsequious hands.

.

"Are you prepared to die?" he demanded abruptly.

The question chimed in so alarmingly with Mr. Budd's thoughts about murder that for a moment it quite threw him off his professional balance.

"I beg your pardon, sir," he stammered, and in the the same moment decided that the man must be a preacher of some kind. He looked rather like it, with his odd, light eyes, his bush of fiery hair and short, jutting chinbeard. Perhaps he even wanted a subscription. That would be hard, when Mr. Budd had already set him down as ninepence, or, with tip, possibly even a shilling.

"Do you do dyeing?" said the man impatiently.

"Oh!" said Mr. Budd, relieved, "yes, sir, certainly, sir."

A stroke of luck, this. Dyeing meant quite a big sum —his mind soared to seven-and-sixpence.

"Good," said the man, sitting down and allowing Mr. Budd to put an apron about his neck. (He was safely gathered in now—he could hardly dart away down the street with a couple of yards of white cotton flapping from his shoulders.)

"Fact is," said the man, "my young lady doesn't like red hair. She says it's conspicuous. The other young ladies in her firm make jokes about it. So, as she's a good bit younger than I am, you see, I like to oblige her, and I was thinking perhaps it could be changed into something quieter, what? Dark brown, now—that's the color she has a fancy for. What do you say?"

It occurred to Mr. Budd that the young ladies might

consider this abrupt change of coat even funnier than the original color, but in the interests of business he agreed that dark brown would be very becoming and a great deal less noticeable than red. Besides, very likely there was no young lady. A woman, he knew, will say frankly that she wants different colored hair for a change, or just to try, or because she fancies it would suit her, but if a man is going to do a silly thing he prefers, if possible, to shuffle the responsibility on to someone else.

"Very well, then," said the customer, "go ahead. And I'm afraid the beard will have to go. My young lady doesn't like beards."

"A great many young ladies don't, sir," said Mr. Budd. "They're not so fashionable nowadays as they used to be. It's very fortunate that you can stand a clean shave very well, sir. You have just the chin for it."

"Do you think so?" said the man, examining himself a little anxiously. "I'm glad to hear it."

"Will you have the mustache off as well, sir?"

"Well, no—no, I think I'll stick to that as long as I'm allowed to, what?" He laughed loudly, and Mr. Budd approvingly noted well-kept teeth and a gold stopping. The customer was obviously ready to spend money on his personal appearance.

In fancy, Mr. Budd saw this well-off and gentlemanly customer advising all his friends to visit "his man"—"wonderful fellow—wonderful—round at the back of Victoria Station—you'd never find it by yourself—only a little place, but he knows what he's about

—I'll write it down for you." It was imperative that there should be no fiasco. Hair-dyes were awkward things—there had been a case in the paper lately.

"I see you have been using a tint before, sir," said Mr. Budd with respect. "Could you tell me—?"

"Eh?" said the man. "Oh, yes—well, fact is, as I said, my fiancée's a good bit younger than I am. As I expect you can see I began to go gray early—my father was just the same—all our family—so I had it touched up—streaky bits restored, you see. But she doesn't take to the color, so I thought, if I have to dye it at all, why not a color she does fancy while we're about it, what?"

It is a common jest among the unthinking that hair-dressers are garrulous. This is their wisdom. The hair-dresser hears many secrets and very many lies. In his discretion he occupies his unruly tongue with the weather and the political situation, lest, restless with inaction, it plunge unbridled into a mad career of inconvenient candor.

Lightly holding forth upon the caprices of the feminine mind, Mr. Budd subjected his customer's locks to the scrutiny of trained eye and fingers. Never—never in the process of nature could hair of that texture and quality have been red. It was naturally black hair, prematurely turned, as some black hair will turn, to a silvery gray. However that was none of his business. He elicited the information he really needed—the name of the dye formerly used, and noted that he would have to be careful. Some dyes do not mix kindly with other dyes.

Chatting pleasantly, Mr. Budd lathered his customer, removed the offending beard, and executed a vigorous shampoo, preliminary to the dyeing process. As he wielded the roaring drier, he reviewed Wimbledon, the Silk-tax and the Summer Time Bill—at that moment threatened with sudden strangulation—and passed naturally on to the Manchester murder.

"The police seem to have given it up as a bad job," said the man.

"Perhaps the reward will liven things up a bit," said Mr. Budd, the thought being naturally uppermost in his mind.

"Oh, there's a reward, is there? I hadn't seen that."

"It's in tonight's paper, sir. Maybe you'd like to have a look at it."

"Thanks, I should."

Mr. Budd left the drier to blow the fiery bush of hair at its own wild will for a moment, while he fetched the *Evening Messenger*. The stranger read the paragraph carefully and Mr. Budd, watching him in the glass, after the disquieting manner of his craft, saw him suddenly draw back his left hand, which was resting carelessly on the arm of the chair, and thrust it under the apron.

But not before Mr. Budd had seen it. Not before he had taken conscious note of the horny, misshapen thumbnail. Many people had such an ugly mark, Mr. Budd told himself hurriedly—there was his friend, Bert Webber, who had sliced the top of his thumb right off in a motorcycle chain—his nail looked very much like that. Mr. Budd thought and thought.

The man glanced up, and the eyes of his reflection became fixed on Mr. Budd's face with a penetrating scrutiny—a horrid warning that the real eyes were steadfastly interrogating the reflection of Mr. Budd.

"Not but what," said Mr. Budd, "the man is safe out of the country, I reckon. They've put it off too late."

The man laughed in a pleasant, conversational way.

"I reckon they have," he said. Mr. Budd wondered whether many men with smashed left thumbs showed a gold left upper eye-tooth. Probably there were hundreds of people like that going about the country. Likewise with silver-gray hair ("may dye same") and aged about forty-three. Undoubtedly.

Mr. Budd folded up the drier and turned off the gas. Mechanically he took up a comb and drew it through the hair that never, never in the process of Nature had been that fiery red.

There came back to him, with an accuracy which quite unnerved him, the exact number and extent of the brutal wounds inflicted upon the Manchester victim —an elderly lady, rather stout, she had been. Glaring through the door, Mr. Budd noticed that his rival over the way had closed. The streets were full of people. How easy it would be—

"Be as quick as you can, won't you?" said the man, a little impatiently, but pleasantly enough. "It's getting late. I'm afraid it will keep you overtime.

"Not at all, sir," said Mr. Budd. "It's of no consequence—not the least."

No—if he tried to bolt out of the door, his terrible customer would leap upon him, drag him back, throttle his cries, and then with one frightful blow like the one he had smashed in his aunt's skull with—

Yet surely Mr. Budd was in a position of advantage. A decided man would do it. He would be out in the street before the customer could disentangle himself from the chair. Mr. Budd began to edge round towards the door.

"What's the matter?" said the customer.

"Just stepping out to look at the time, sir," said Mr. Budd, meekly pausing. (Yet he might have done it then, if he only had the courage to make the first swift step that would give the game away.)

"It's five-and-twenty past eight," said the man, "by tonight's broadcast. I'll pay extra for the overtime."

"Not on any account," said Mr. Budd. Too late now, he couldn't make another effort. He vividly saw himself tripping on the threshold—falling—the terrible fist lifted to smash him into a pulp. Or, perhaps, under the familiar white apron, the disfigured hand was actually clutching a pistol.

Mr. Budd retreated to the back of the shop, collecting his materials. If only he had been quicker—more like a detective in a book—he would have observed that thumbnail, that tooth, put two and two together, and run out to give the alarm while the man's beard was wet and soapy and his face buried in the towel. Or he could have dabbed lather in his eyes—nobody could possibly commit a murder or even run away down the street with his eyes full of soap.

Even now—Mr. Budd took down a bottle, shook his head and put it back on the shelf—even now, was it really too late? Why could he not take a bold course? He had only to open a razor, go quietly up behind the unsuspecting man and say in a firm, loud, convincing voice: "William Strickland, put up your hands. Your life is at my mercy. Stand up till I take your gun away. Now walk straight out to the nearest policeman." Surely, in his position, that was what Sherlock Holmes would do.

But as Mr. Budd returned with a little trayful of requirements, it was borne in upon him that he was not of the stuff of which great man-hunters are made. For he could not seriously see that attempt "coming off." Because if he held the razor to the man's throat and said: "Put up your hands," the man would probably merely catch him by the wrists and take the razor away. And greatly as Mr. Budd feared his customer unarmed, he felt it would be a perfect crescendo of madness to put a razor in his hands.

Or, supposing he said, "Put up your hands," and the man just said, "I won't." What was he to do next? To cut his throat then and there would be murder, even if Mr. Budd could possibly have brought himself to do such a thing. They could not remain there, fixed in one position, till the boy came to do out the shop in the morning.

Perhaps the policeman would notice the light on and the door unfastened and come in? Then he would say,

"I congratulate you, Mr. Budd, on having captured a very dangerous criminal." But supposing the policeman didn't happen to notice—and Mr. Budd would have to stand all the time, and he would get exhausted and his attention would relax, and then—

After all, Mr. Budd wasn't called upon to arrest the man himself. "Information leading to arrest"— those were the words. He would be able to tell them the wanted man had been there, that he would now have dark brown hair and mustache and no beard. He might even shadow him when he left—he might—

It was at this moment that the great Inspiration came to Mr. Budd.

As he fetched a bottle from the glass-fronted case he remembered with odd vividness, an old-fashioned wooden paper-knife that had belonged to his mother. Between sprigs of blue forget-me-not, hand-painted, it bore the inscription "Knowledge is Power."

A strange freedom and confidence were vouchsafed to Mr. Budd; his mind was alert; he removed the razors with an easy, natural movement, and made nonchalant conversation as he skillfully applied the dark-brown tint.

The streets were less crowded when Mr. Budd let his customer out. He watched the tall figure cross Grosvenor Place and climb on to a 24 bus.

"But that was only his artfulness," said Mr. Budd, as he put on his hat and coat and extinguished the lights carefully, "he'll take another at Victoria, like as not, and be making tracks from Charing Cross or Waterloo."

He closed the shop door, shook it, as was his wont, to make sure that the lock had caught properly, and in his turn made his way, by means of a 24, to the top of Whitehall.

The policeman was a little condescending at first when Mr. Budd demanded to see "somebody very high up," but finding the little barber insist so earnestly that he had news of the Manchester murderer, and that there wasn't any time to lose, he consented to pass him through.

Mr. Budd was interviewed first by an important-looking inspector in uniform, who listened very politely to his story and made him repeat very carefully about the gold tooth and the thumbnail and the hair which had been black before it was gray or red and now dark-brown.

The inspector then touched a bell, and said, "Perkins, I think Sir Andrew would like to see this gentleman at once," and he was taken to another room, where sat a very shrewd, genial gentleman in mufti, who heard him with even greater attention, and called in another inspector to listen too, and to take down a very exact description of—yes, surely the undoubted William Strickland as he now appeared.

"But there's one thing more," said Mr. Budd—"and I'm sure to goodness," he added, "I hope, sir, it is the right man, because if it isn't it'll be the ruin of me—"

He crushed his soft hat into an agitated ball as he leaned across the table, breathlessly uttering the story of his great betrayal.

"Tzee—z-z-z—tzee—tzee—z-z—tzee—z-z—"
"Dzoo—dz-dz-dz—dzoo—dz—dzoo—dzoo—dz"
"Tzee—z—z."

The fingers of the wireless operator on the packet *Miranda* bound for Ostend moved swiftly as they jotted down the messages of the buzzing wireless mosquito-swarms.

One of them made him laugh.

"The Old Man'd better have this, I suppose," he said.

The Old Man scratched his head when he read and rang a little bell for the steward. The steward ran down to the little round office where the purser was counting his money and checking it before he locked it away for the night. On receiving the Old Man's message, the purser put the money quickly into the safe, picked up the passenger list and departed aft. There was a short consultation, and the bell was rung again—this time to summon the head steward.

"Tzee—z-z—tzeez-z-z—tzee—tzee—z—tzee."

All down the Channel, all over the North Sea, up to the Mersey Docks, out into the Atlantic soared the busy mosquito-swarms. In ship after ship the wireless operator sent his message to the captain, the captain sent for the purser, the purser sent for the head steward and the head steward called his staff about him. Huge liners, little packets, destroyers, sumptuous private yachts—every floating thing that carried aerials—every port in England, France, Holland, Germany, Denmark, Norway, every police center that could interpret the mosquito message, heard, between laughter and excitement, the tale of Mr. Budd's betrayal. Two Boy Scouts at Croydon, practicing their Morse with a home-made valve set, decoded it laboriously into an exercise book.

"Cripes," said Jim to George, "what a joke! D'you think they'll get the beggar?"

The *Miranda* docked at Ostend at 7 A.M. A man burst hurriedly into the cabin where the wireless operator was just taking off his headphones.

"Here!" he cried; "this is to go. There's something up and the Old Man's sent over for the police. The Consul's coming on board."

The wireless operator groaned, and switched on his valves.

"Tzee—z—tzee—" a message to the English police.

"Man on board answering to description. Ticket booked name of Watson. Has locked himself in cabin and refuses to come out. Insists on having hairdresser sent out to him. Have communicated Ostend police. Await instructions."

The Old Man with sharp words and authoritative gestures cleared a way through the excited little knot of people gathered about First Class Cabin No. 36. Several passengers had got wind of "something up." Magnificently he herded them away to the gangway with their bags and suitcases. Sternly he bade the stewards and the boy, who stood gaping with his hands full of breakfast dishes, to stand away from the door. Terribly he commanded them to hold their tongues. Four or five sailors stood watchfully at his side. In the restored silence, the passenger in No. 36 could be heard pacing up and down the narrow cabin, moving things, clatter-ing, splashing water.

Presently came steps overhead. Somebody arrived, with a message. The Old Man nodded. Six pairs of Belgian police boots came tip-toeing down the com-panion. The Old Man glanced at the official paper held out to him and nodded again.

"Ready?"

"Yes."

The Old Man knocked at the door of No. 36.

"Who is it?" cried a harsh, sharp voice.

"The barber is here, sir, that you sent for."

"Ah!" There was relief in the tone. "Send him in alone if you please. I—I have had an accident."

"Yes, sir."

At the sound of the bolt being cautiously withdrawn, the Old Man stepped forward. The door opened a chink, and was slammed to again, but the Old Man's boot was firmly wedged against the jamb. The police-men surged forward. There was a yelp and a shot which smashed harmlessly through the window of the first-class saloon, and the passenger was brought out.

"Strike me pink!" shrieked the boy, "strike me pink if he ain't gone green in the night!"

Green!

Not for nothing had Mr. Budd studied the intricate mutual reactions of chemical dyes. In the pride of his knowledge he had set a mark on his man, to mark him out from the billions of this overpopulated world. Was there a port in all Christendom where a murderer might slip away, with every hair on him green as a parrot—green mustache, green eyebrows, and that thick, springing shock of hair, vivid, flaring midsummer green?

Mr. Budd got his £500. The *Evening Messenger* published the full story of his great betrayal. He trembled, fearing this sinister fame. Surely no one would ever come to him again.

On the next morning an enormous blue limousine rolled up to his door, to the immense admiration of Wilton Street. A lady, magnificent in musquash and diamonds, swept into the saloon.

"You are Mr. Budd, aren't you?" she cried. "The great Mr. Budd? Isn't it too wonderful? And now, dear Mr. Budd, you must do me a favor. You must dye my hair green, at once. Now. I want to be able to say I'm the very first to be done by you. I'm the Duchess of Winchester, and that awful Melcaster woman is chasing me down the street—the cat!"

If you want it done, I can give you the number of Mr. Budd's parlors in Bond Street. But I understand it is a terribly expensive process.

JACQUES FUTRELLE

. . . was born in Georgia in 1875. Thirty-seven years later, he perished in the sinking of the Titanic. *He was the first American after Poe to write any important detective stories.*

Futrelle's peppery-tempered detective, known as The Thinking Machine, had no time for fools, and is one of the most fascinating characters in our literature. In spite of the fact that he becomes downright irritable at times, The Thinking Machine's outspokenness has a way of making him the more admired and liked by his readers.

The Thinking Machine's superb feat in meeting the challenge of "The Problem of Cell 13" makes this a classic among mystery stories.

The Thinking Machine has only his wits to solve

THE PROBLEM
OF CELL 13

Can he escape from a concrete jail?

PRACTICALLY all those letters remaining in the alphabet after Augustus S. F. X. Van Dusen was named were afterward acquired by that gentleman in the course of a brilliant scientific career, and, being honorably acquired, were tacked on to the other end. His name, therefore, taken with all that belonged to it, was a wonderfully imposing structure. He was a Ph.D., an LL.D., an F.R.S., an M.D., and an M.D.S. He was also some other things—just what he himself couldn't say—through recognition of his ability by various foreign educational and scientific institutions.

In appearance he was no less striking than in nomenclature. He was slender with the droop of the student in his thin shoulders and the pallor of a close,

sedentary life on his clean-shaven face. His eyes wore
a perpetual, forbidding squint—of a man who studies
little things—and when they could be seen at all
through his thick spectacles, were mere slits of watery
blue. But above his eyes was his most striking feature.
This was a tall, broad brow, almost abnormal in height
and width, crowned by a heavy shock of bushy, yellow
hair. All these things conspired to give him a peculiar,
almost grotesque, personality.

Professor Van Dusen was remotely German. For
generations his ancestors had been noted in the sciences; he was the logical result, the master mind. First
and above all he was a logician. At least thirty-five
years of the half-century or so of his existence had
been devoted exclusively to proving that two and two
always equal four, except in unusual cases, where they
equal three or five, as the case may be. He stood broadly
on the general proposition that all things that start
must go somewhere, and was able to bring the concentrated mental force of his forefathers to bear on a
given problem. Incidentally it may be remarked that
Professor Van Dusen wore a No. 8 hat.

The world at large had heard vaguely of Professor
Van Dusen as The Thinking Machine. It was a newspaper catch-phrase applied to him at the time of a
remarkable exhibition at chess; he had demonstrated
then that a stranger to the game might, by the force
of inevitable logic, defeat a champion who had devoted a lifetime to its study. The Thinking Machine!
Perhaps that more nearly described him than all his

honorary initials, for he spent week after week, month after month, in the seclusion of his small laboratory from which had gone forth thoughts that staggered scientific associates and deeply stirred the world at large.

It was only occasionally that The Thinking Machine had visitors, and these were usually men who, themselves high in the sciences, dropped in to argue a point and perhaps convince themselves. Two of these men, Dr. Charles Ransome and Alfred Fielding, called one evening to discuss some theory which is not of consequence here.

"Such a thing is impossible," declared Dr. Ransome emphatically, in the course of the conversation.

"Nothing is impossible," declared The Thinking Machine with equal emphasis. He always spoke petulantly. "The mind is master of all things. When science fully recognizes that fact a great advance will have been made."

Dr. Ransome laughed tolerantly.

"I've heard you say such things before," he said. "But they mean nothing. Mind may be master of matter, but it hasn't yet found a way to apply itself. There are some things that can't be *thought* out of existence, or rather which would not yield to any amount of thinking."

"What, for instance?" demanded The Thinking Machine.

Dr. Ransome was thoughtful for a moment as he smoked. "Well, say prison walls," he replied. "No man can *think* himself out of a cell. If he could, there would be no prisoners."

"A man can so apply his brain and ingenuity that he can leave a cell, which is the same thing," snapped The Thinking Machine.

Dr. Ransome was slightly amused.

"Let's suppose a case," he said, after a moment. "Take a cell where prisoners under sentence of death are confined—men who are desperate and, maddened by fear, would take any chance to escape—suppose you were locked in such a cell. Could you escape?"

"Certainly," declared The Thinking Machine.

"Of course," said Mr. Fielding, who entered the conversation for the first time, "you might wreck the cell with an explosive—but inside, a prisoner, you couldn't have that."

"There would be nothing of that kind," said The Thinking Machine. "You might treat me precisely as you treated prisoners under sentence of death, and I would leave the cell."

"Not unless you entered it with tools prepared to get out," said Dr. Ransome.

The Thinking Machine was visibly annoyed and his blue eyes snapped.

"Lock me in any cell in any prison anywhere at any time, wearing only what is necessary, and I'll escape in a week," he declared, sharply.

Dr. Ransome sat up straight in the chair, interested. Mr. Fielding lighted a new cigar.

"You mean you could actually *think* yourself out?"

asked Dr. Ransome. He looked incredulous.

"I would get out," was the response.

"Are you serious?"

"Certainly I am serious."

Dr. Ransome and Mr. Fielding were silent for a long time.

"Would you be willing to try it?" asked Mr. Fielding, finally.

"Certainly," said Professor Van Dusen, and there was a trace of irony in his voice. "I have done more asinine things than that to convince other men of less important truths."

The tone was offensive and there was an undercurrent strongly resembling anger on both sides. Of course it was an absurd thing, but Professor Van Dusen reiterated his willingness to undertake the escape and it was decided upon.

"To begin now," added Dr. Ransome.

"I'd prefer that it begin to-morrow," said The Thinking Machine, "because—"

"No, now," said Mr. Fielding, flatly. "You **are** arrested, figuratively, of course, without any warning locked in a cell with no chance to communicate with friends, and left there with identically the same care and attention that would be given to a man under sentence of death. Are you willing?"

"All right, now, then," said The Thinking Machine, and he arose.

"Say, the death-cell in Chisholm Prison."

"The death-cell in Chisholm Prison."

"And what will you wear?"

"As little as possible," said The Thinking Machine. "Shoes, stockings, trousers and a shirt."

"You will permit yourself to be searched, of course?"

"I am to be treated precisely as all prisoners are treated," said The Thinking Machine. "No more attention and no less."

There were some preliminaries to be arranged in the matter of obtaining permission for the test, but all three were influential men and everything was done satisfactorily by telephone, albeit the prison commissioners, to whom the experiment was explained on purely scientific grounds, were sadly bewildered. Professor Van Dusen would be the most distinguished prisoner they had ever entertained.

When The Thinking Machine had donned those things which he was to wear during his incarceration he called the little old woman who was his housekeeper, cook and maid-servant all in one.

"Martha," he said, "it is now twenty-seven minutes past nine o'clock. I am going away. One week from to-night, at half-past nine, these gentlemen and one, possibly two, others will take supper with me here. Remember Dr. Ransome is very fond of artichokes."

The three men were driven to Chisholm Prison, where the warden was awaiting them, having been informed of the matter by telephone. He understood merely that the eminent Professor Van Dusen was to be his prisoner, if he could keep him, for one week;

that he had committed no crime, but that he was to be treated as all other prisoners were treated.

"Search him," instructed Dr. Ransome.

The Thinking Machine was searched. Nothing was found on him; the pockets of the trousers were empty; the white, stiff-bosomed shirt had no pocket. The shoes and stockings were removed, examined, then replaced. As he watched all these preliminaries—the rigid search —and noted the pitiful, childlike physical weakness of the man, the colorless face, and the thin, white hands, Dr. Ransome almost regretted his part in the affair.

"Are you sure you want to do this?" he asked.

"Would you be convinced if I did not?" inquired The Thinking Machine in turn.

"No."

"All right. I'll do it."

What sympathy Dr. Ransome had was dissipated by the tone. It nettled him, and he resolved to see the experiment to the end; it would be a stinging reproof to egotism.

"It will be impossible for him to communicate with any one outside?" he asked.

"Absolutely impossible," replied the warden. "He will not be permitted writing materials of any sort."

"And your jailers, would they deliver a message from him?"

"Not one word, directly or indirectly," said the warden. "You may rest assured of that. They will report anything he might say or turn over to me anything he might give them."

"That seems entirely satisfactory," said Mr. Fielding, who was frankly interested in the problem.

"Of course, in the event he fails," said Dr. Ransome, "and asks for his liberty, you understand you are to set him free?"

"I understand," replied the warden.

The Thinking Machine stood listening, but had nothing to say until this was all ended, then:

"I should like to make three small requests. You may grant them or not, as you wish."

"No special favors, now," warned Mr. Fielding.

"I am asking none," was the stiff response. "I would like to have some tooth powder—buy it yourself to see that it is tooth powder—and I should like to have one five-dollar and two ten-dollar bills."

Dr. Ransome, Mr. Fielding and the warden exchanged astonished glances. They were not surprised at the request for tooth powder, but were at the request for money.

"Is there any man with whom our friend would come in contact that he could bribe with twenty-five dollars?" asked Dr. Ransome of the warden.

"Not for twenty-five hundred dollars," was the positive reply.

"Well, let him have them," said Mr. Fielding. "I think they are harmless enough."

"And what is the third request?" asked Dr. Ransome.

"I should like to have my shoes polished."

Again the astonished glances were exchanged. This last request was the height of absurdity, so they agreed to it. These things all being attended to, The Thinking Machine was led back into the prison from which he had undertaken to escape.

"Here is Cell 13," said the warden, stopping three doors down the steel corridor. "This is where we keep condemned murderers. No one can leave it without my permission; and no one in it can communicate with the outside. I'll stake my reputation on that. It's only three doors back of my office and I can readily hear any unusual noise."

"Will this cell do, gentlemen?" asked The Thinking Machine. There was a touch of irony in his voice.

"Admirably," was the reply.

The heavy steel door was thrown open, there was a great scurrying and scampering of tiny feet, and The Thinking Machine passed into the gloom of the cell. Then the door was closed and double locked by the warden.

"What is that noise in there?" asked Dr. Ransome, through the bars.

"Rats—dozens of them," replied The Thinking Machine, tersely.

The three men, with final good nights, were turning away when The Thinking Machine called:

"What time is it exactly, warden?"

"Eleven seventeen," replied the warden.

"Thanks. I will join you gentlemen in your office at half-past eight o'clock one week from to-night," said The Thinking Machine.

"And if you do not?"

"There is no 'if' about it."

II

Chisholm Prison was a great, spreading structure of granite, four stories in all, which stood in the center of acres of open space. It was surrounded by a wall of solid masonry eighteen feet high, and so smoothly finished inside and out as to offer no foothold to a climber, no matter how expert. Atop of this wall, as a further precaution, was a five-foot fence of steel rods, each terminating in a keen point. This fence in itself marked an absolute deadline between freedom and imprisonment, for, even if a man escaped from his cell, it would seem impossible for him to pass the wall.

The yard, which on all sides of the prison building was twenty-five feet wide, that being the distance from the building to the wall, was by day an exercise ground for those prisoners to whom was granted the boon of occasional semi-liberty. But that was not for those in Cell 13.

At all times of the day there were armed guards in the yard, four of them, one patrolling each side of the prison building. By night the yard was almost as brilliantly lighted as by day. On each of the four sides was a great arc light which rose above the prison wall and gave to the guards a clear sight. The lights, too, brightly illuminated the spiked top of the wall. The wires which fed the arc lights ran up the side of the prison building on insulators and from the top story led out to the poles supporting the arc lights.

All these things were seen and comprehended by The Thinking Machine, who was only enabled to see out his closely barred cell window by standing on his bed. This was on the morning following his incarceration. He gathered, too, that the river lay over there beyond the wall somewhere, because he heard faintly the pulsation of a motor boat and high up in the air saw a river bird. From that same direction came the shouts of boys at play and the occasional crack of a batted ball. He knew then that between the prison wall and the river was an open space, a playground.

Chisholm Prison was regarded as absolutely safe. No man had ever escaped from it. The Thinking Machine, from his perch on the bed, seeing what he saw, could readily understand why. The walls of the cell, though built he judged twenty years before, were perfectly solid, and the window bars of new iron had not a shadow of rust on them. The window itself, even with the bars out, would be a difficult mode of egress because it was small.

Yet, seeing these things, The Thinking Machine was not discouraged. Instead, he thoughtfully squinted at the great arc light—there was bright sunlight now—and traced with his eyes the wire which led from it to the building. That electric wire, he reasoned, must come down the side of the building not a great distance from his cell. That might be worth knowing.

Cell 13 was on the same floor with the offices of the

prison—that is, not in the basement, not yet upstairs.
There were only four steps up to the office floor, therefore the level of the floor must be only three or four
feet above the ground. He couldn't see the ground
directly beneath the window, but he could see it further out toward the wall. It would be an easy drop
from the window. Well and good.

Then The Thinking Machine fell to remembering
how he had come to the cell. First, there was the outside guard's booth, a part of the wall. There were two
heavily barred gates there, both of steel. At this gate
was one man always on guard. He admitted persons
to the prison after much clanking of keys and locks,
and let them out when ordered to do so. The warden's
office was in the prison building, and in order to reach
that official from the prison yard one had to pass a gate
of solid steel with only a peep-hole in it. Then coming
from that inner office to Cell 13, where he was now,
one must pass a heavy wooden door and two steel
doors into the corridors of the prison; and always there
was the double-locked door to Cell 13 to reckon with.

There were then, The Thinking Machine recalled,
seven doors to be overcome before one could pass from
Cell 13 into the outer world, a free man. But against
this was the fact that he was rarely interrupted. A
jailer appeared at his cell door at six in the morning
with a breakfast of prison fare; he would come again
at noon, and again at six in the afternoon. At nine
o'clock at night would come the inspection tour. That
would be all.

"It's admirably arranged, this prison system," was the mental tribute paid by The Thinking Machine. "I'll have to study it a little when I get out. I had no idea there was such great care exercised in the prisons."

There was nothing, positively nothing, in his cell, except his iron bed, so firmly put together that no man could tear it to pieces save with sledges or a file. He had neither of these. There was not even a chair, or a small table, or a bit of crockery. Nothing! The jailer stood by when he ate, then took away the wooden spoon and bowl which he had used.

One by one these things sank into the brain of The Thinking Machine. When the last possibility had been considered he began an examination of his cell. From the roof, down the walls on all sides, he examined the stones and the cement between them. He stamped over the floor carefully time after time, but it was cement, perfectly solid. After the examination he sat on the edge of the iron bed and was lost in thought for a long time. For Professor Augustus S. F. X. Van Dusen, The Thinking Machine, had something to think about.

He was disturbed by a rat, which ran across his feet, then scampered away into a dark corner of the cell, frightened at its own daring. After a while The Thinking Machine, squinting steadily into the darkness of the corner where the rat had gone, was able to make out in the gloom many little beady eyes staring at him. He counted six pair, and there were perhaps others; he didn't see very well.

Then The Thinking Machine, from his seat on the

bed, noticed for the first time the bottom of his cell door. There was an opening there of two inches between the steel bar and the floor. Still looking steadily at this opening, The Thinking Machine backed suddenly into the corner where he had seen the beady eyes. There was a great scampering of tiny feet, several squeaks of frightened rodents, and then silence.

None of the rats had gone out the door, yet there were none in the cell. Therefore there must be another way out of the cell, however small. The Thinking Machine, on hands and knees, started a search for this spot, feeling in the darkness with his long, slender fingers.

At last his search was rewarded. He came upon a small opening in the floor, level with the cement. It was perfectly round and somewhat larger than a silver dollar. This was the way the rats had gone. He put his fingers deep into the opening; it seemed to be a disused drainage pipe and was dry and dusty.

Having satisfied himself on this point, he sat on the bed again for an hour, then made another inspection of his surroundings through the small cell window. One of the outside guards stood directly opposite, beside the wall, and happened to be looking at the window of Cell 13 when the head of The Thinking Machine appeared. But the scientist didn't notice the guard.

Noon came and the jailer appeared with the prison dinner of repulsively plain food. At home The Thinking Machine merely ate to live; here he took what was offered without comment. Occasionally he spoke to the jailer who stood outside the door watching him.

"Any improvements made here in the last few years?" he asked.

"Nothing particularly," replied the jailer. "New wall was built four years ago."

"Anything done to the prison proper?"

"Painted the woodwork outside, and I believe about seven years ago a new system of plumbing was put in."

"Ah!" said the prisoner. "How far is the river over there?"

"About three hundred feet. The boys have a baseball ground between the wall and the river."

The Thinking Machine had nothing further to say just then, but when the jailer was ready to go he asked for some water.

"I get very thirsty here," he explained. "Would it be possible for you to leave a little water in a bowl for me?"

"I'll ask the warden," replied the jailer, and he went away.

Half an hour later he returned with water in a small earthen bowl.

"The warden says you may keep this bowl," he informed the prisoner. "But you must show it to me when I ask for it. If it is broken, it will be the last."

"Thank you," said The Thinking Machine. "I shan't break it."

The jailer went on about his duties. For just the fraction of a second it seemed that The Thinking Machine wanted to ask a question, but he didn't.

Two hours later this same jailer, in passing the door of Cell No. 13, heard a noise inside and stopped. The Thinking Machine was down on his hands and knees in a corner of the cell, and from that same corner came several frightened squeaks. The jailer looked on interestedly.

"Ah, I've got you," he heard the prisoner say.

"Got what?" he asked, sharply.

"One of these rats," was the reply. "See?" And between the scientist's long fingers the jailer saw a small gray rat struggling. The prisoner brought it over to the light and looked at it closely. "It's a water rat," he said.

"Ain't you got anything better to do than to catch rats?" asked the jailer.

"It's disgraceful that they should be here at all," was the irritated reply. "Take this one away and kill it. There are dozens more where it came from."

The jailer took the wriggling, squirmy rodent and flung it down on the floor violently. It gave one squeak and lay still. Later he reported the incident to the warden, who only smiled.

Still later that afternoon the outside guard on Cell 13 side of the prison looked up again at the window and saw the prisoner looking out. He saw a hand raised to the barred window and then something white fluttered to the ground directly under the window of Cell 13. It was a little roll of linen, evidently of white shirting material; tied around it was a five-dollar bill.

With a grim smile he took the linen roll and the five-dollar bill to the warden's office. There together they deciphered something which was written on it with a queer sort of ink, frequently blurred. On the outside was this:

"Finder of this please deliver to Dr. Charles Ransome."

"Ah," said the warden, with a chuckle. "Plan of escape number one has gone wrong." Then, as an afterthought: "But why did he address it to Dr. Ransome?"

"And where did he get the pen and ink to write with?" asked the guard.

The warden looked at the guard and the guard looked at the warden. There was no apparent solution of that mystery. The warden studied the writing carefully, then shook his head.

"Well, let's see what he was going to say to Dr. Ransome," he said at length, still puzzled, and he unrolled the inner piece of linen.

"Well, if that—what—what do you think of that?" he asked, dazed.

The guard took the bit of linen and read this:
"Epa cseot d'net niiy awe htto n'si sih. 'T.'"

III

The warden spent an hour wondering what sort of a cipher it was, and half an hour wondering why his prisoner should attempt to communicate with Dr. Ransome, who was the cause of him being there. After this the warden devoted some thought to the question of where the prisoner got writing materials, and what sort of writing materials he had. With the idea of illuminating this point, he examined the linen again. It was a torn part of a white shirt and had ragged edges.

Now it was possible to account for the linen, but what the prisoner had used to write with was another matter. The warden knew it would have been impossible for him to have either pen or pencil, and, besides, neither pen nor pencil had been used in this writing. What, then? The warden decided to investigate personally. The Thinking Machine was his prisoner; he had orders to hold his prisoners; if this one sought escape by sending cipher messages to persons outside, he would stop it, as he would have stopped it in the case of any other prisoner.

The warden went back to Cell 13 and found The Thinking Machine on his hands and knees on the floor, engaged in nothing more alarming than catching rats. The prisoner heard the warden's step and turned to him quickly.

"It's disgraceful," he snapped, "these rats. There are scores of them."

"Other men have been able to stand them," said the warden. "Here is another shirt for you—let me have the one you have on."

"Why?" demanded The Thinking Machine, quickly. His tone was hardly natural, his manner suggested actual perturbation and annoyance.

"You have attempted to communicate with Dr. Ransome," said the warden severely. "As my prisoner, it is my duty to put a stop to it."

The Thinking Machine was silent for a moment.

"All right," he said, finally. "Do your duty."

The warden smiled grimly. The prisoner arose from the floor and removed the white shirt, putting on instead a striped convict shirt the warden had brought. The warden took the white shirt eagerly, and then and there compared the pieces of linen on which was written the cipher with certain torn places in the shirt. The Thinking Machine looked on curiously.

"The guard brought *you* those, then?"—he asked.

"He certainly did," replied the warden triumphantly. "And that ends your first attempt to escape."

The Thinking Machine watched the warden as he, by comparison, established to his own satisfaction that only two pieces of linen had been torn from the white shirt.

"What did you write this with?" demanded the warden.

"I should think it a part of your duty to find out," said The Thinking Machine, irritably.

The warden started to say some harsh things, then restrained himself and made a minute search of the cell and of the prisoner instead. He found absolutely nothing; not even a match or toothpick which might have been used for a pen. The same mystery surrounded the fluid with which the cipher had been written. Although the warden left Cell 13 visibly annoyed, he took the torn shirt in triumph.

"Well, writing notes on a shirt won't get him out, that's certain," he told himself with some complacency. He put the linen scraps into his desk to await developments. "If that man escapes from that cell I'll—hang it —I'll resign."

On the third day of his incarceration The Thinking Machine openly attempted to bribe his way out. The jailer had brought his dinner and was leaning against the barred door, waiting, when The Thinking Machine began the conversation.

"The drainage pipes of the prison lead to the river, don't they?" he asked.

"Yes," said the jailer.

"I suppose they are very small?"

"Too small to crawl through, if that's what you're thinking about," was the grinning response.

There was silence until The Thinking Machine finished his meal. Then:

"You know I'm not a criminal, don't you?"

"Yes."

"And that I've a perfect right to be freed if I demanded it?"

"Yes."

"Well, I came here believing that I could make my escape," said the prisoner, and his squint eyes studied the face of the jailer. "Would you consider a financial reward for aiding me to escape?"

The jailer, who happened to be an honest man, looked at the slender, weak figure of the prisoner, at the large head with its mass of yellow hair, and was almost sorry.

"I guess prisons like these were not built for the likes of you to get out of," he said, at last.

"But would you consider a proposition to help me get out?" the prisoner insisted, almost beseechingly.

"No," said the jailer, shortly.

"Five hundred dollars," urged The Thinking Machine. "I am not a criminal."

"No," said the jailer.

"A thousand?"

"No," again said the jailer, and he started away hurriedly to escape further temptation. Then he turned back. "If you should give me ten thousand dollars I couldn't get you out. You'd have to pass through seven doors, and I only have the keys to two."

Then he told the warden all about it.

"Plan number two fails," said the warden, smiling grimly. "First a cipher, then bribery."

When the jailer was on his way to Cell 13 at six o'clock, again bearing food to The Thinking Machine, he paused, startled by the unmistakable scrape, scrape of steel against steel. It stopped at the sound of his steps, then craftily the jailer, who was beyond the prisoner's range of vision, resumed his tramping, the sound being apparently that of a man going away from Cell 13. As a matter of fact he was in the same spot.

After a moment there came again the steady scrape,

scrape, and the jailer crept cautiously on tiptoes to the door and peered between the bars. The Thinking Machine was standing on the iron bed working at the bars of the little window. He was using a file, judging from the backward and forward swing of his arms.

Cautiously the jailer crept back to the office, summoned the warden in person, and they returned to Cell 13 on tiptoes. The steady scrape was still audible. The warden listened to satisfy himself and then suddenly appeared at the door.

"Well?" he demanded, and there was a smile on his face.

The Thinking Machine glanced back from his perch on the bed and leaped suddenly to the floor, making frantic efforts to hide something. The warden went in, with hand extended.

"Give it up," he said.

"No," said the prisoner, sharply.

"Come, give it up," urged the warden. "I don't want to have to search you again."

"No," repeated the prisoner.

"What was it, a file?" asked the warden.

The Thinking Machine was silent and stood squinting at the warden with something very nearly approaching disappointment on his face—nearly, but not quite. The warden was almost sympathetic.

"Plan number three fails, eh?" he asked, good-naturedly. "Too bad, isn't it?"

The prisoner didn't say.

"Search him," instructed the warden.

The jailer searched the prisoner carefully. At last, artfully concealed in the waistband of the trousers, he found a piece of steel about two inches long, with one side curved like a half moon.

"Ah," said the warden, as he received it from the jailer. "From your shoe heel," and he smiled pleasantly.

The jailer continued his search and on the other side of the trousers waistband found another piece of steel identical with the first. The edge showed where they had been worn against the bars of the window.

"You couldn't saw a way through those bars with these," said the warden.

"I could have," said The Thinking Machine firmly.

"In six months, perhaps," said the warden, good-naturedly.

The warden shook his head slowly as he gazed into the highly flushed face of his prisoner.

"Ready to give it up?" he asked.

"I haven't started yet," was the prompt reply.

Then came another exhaustive search of the cell. Carefully the two men went over it, finally turning out the bed and searching that. Nothing. The warden in person climbed upon the bed and examined the bars of the window where the prisoner had been sawing.

"Just made it a little bright by hard rubbing," he said to the prisoner, who stood looking on with a somewhat crestfallen air. The warden grasped the iron bars in his strong hands and tried to shake them. They were immovable, set firmly in the solid granite. He examined each in turn and found them all satisfactory. Finally he climbed down from the bed.

"Give it up, professor," he advised.

The Thinking Machine shook his head and the warden and jailer passed on again. As they disappeared down the corridor The Thinking Machine sat on the edge of the bed with his head in his hands.

"He's crazy to try to get out of that cell," commented the jailer.

"Of course he can't get out," said the warden. "But he's clever. I would like to know what he wrote that cipher with."

*   *   *   *

It was four o'clock next morning when an awful, heart-rending shriek of terror resounded through the great prison. It came from a cell, somewhere about the center, and its tone told a tale of horror, agony, terrible fear. The warden heard and with three of his men rushed into the long corridor leading to Cell 13.

IV

As they ran there came again that awful cry. It died away in a sort of wail. The white faces of prisoners appeared at cell doors upstairs and down, staring out wonderingly, frightened.

"It's that fool in Cell 13," grumbled the warden.

He stopped and stared in as one of the jailers flashed a lantern. "That fool in Cell 13" lay comfortably on his cot, flat on his back with his mouth open, snoring. Even as they looked there came again the piercing cry, from somewhere above. The warden's face blanched a little as he started up the stairs. There on the top floor he found a man in Cell 43, directly above Cell 13, but two floors higher, cowering in a corner of his cell.

"What's the matter?" demanded the warden.

"Thank God you've come," exclaimed the prisoner, and he cast himself against the bars of his cell.

"What is it?" demanded the warden again.

He threw open the door and went in. The prisoner dropped on his knees and clasped the warden about the body. His face was white with terror, his eyes were widely distended, and he was shuddering. His hands, icy cold, clutched at the warden's.

"Take me out of this cell, please take me out," he pleaded.

"What's the matter with you, anyhow?" insisted the warden, impatiently.

"I heard something—something," said the prisoner, and his eyes roved nervously around the cell.

"What did you hear?"

"I—I can't tell you," stammered the prisoner. Then, in a sudden burst of terror: "Take me out of this cell— put me anywhere—but take me out of here."

The warden and the three jailers exchanged glances.

"Who is this fellow? What's he accused of?" asked the warden.

"Joseph Ballard," said one of the jailers. "He's accused of throwing acid in a woman's face. She died from it."

"But they can't prove it," gasped the prisoner. "They can't prove it. Please put me in some other cell."

He was still clinging to the warden, and that official threw his arms off roughly. Then for a time he stood looking at the cowering wretch, who seemed possessed of all the wild, unreasoning terror of a child.

"Look here, Ballard," said the warden, finally, "if you heard anything, I want to know what it was. Now tell me."

"I can't, I can't," was the reply. He was sobbing.

"Where did it come from?"

"I don't know. Everywhere—nowhere. I just heard it."

"What was it—a voice?"

"Please don't make me answer," pleaded the prisoner.

"You must answer," said the warden, sharply.

"It was a voice—but—but it wasn't human," was the sobbing reply.

"Voice, but not human?" repeated the warden, puzzled.

"It sounded muffled and—and far away—and ghostly," explained the man.

"Did it come from inside or outside the prison?"

"It didn't seem to come from anywhere—it was just here, here, there, everywhere. I heard it. I heard it."

For an hour the warden tried to get the story, but Ballard had become suddenly obstinate and would say nothing—only pleaded to be placed in another cell, or to have one of the jailers remain near him until day-light. These requests were gruffly refused.

"And see here," said the warden, in conclusion, "if there's any more of this screaming I'll put you in the padded cell."

Then the warden went his way, a sadly puzzled man. Ballard sat at his cell door until daylight, his face drawn and white with terror, pressed against the bars, and looked out into the prison with wide, staring eyes.

That day, the fourth since the incarceration of The Thinking Machine, was enlivened considerably by the volunteer prisoner, who spent most of his time at the little window of his cell. He began proceedings by throwing another piece of linen down to the guard, who picked it up dutifully and took it to the warden. On it was written:

"Only three days more."

The warden was in no way surprised at what he read; he understood that The Thinking Machine meant only three days more of his imprisonment, and he regarded the note as a boast. But how was the thing written? Where had The Thinking Machine found this new piece of linen? Where? How? He carefully examined the linen. It was white, of fine texture, shirting material. He took the shirt which he had taken and carefully fitted the two diagonal pieces of the linen to the torn places. The third piece was entirely superfluous; it didn't fit anywhere, and yet it was unmistakably the same goods.

"And where—where does he get anything to write

with?" demanded the warden of the world at large.

Still later on the fourth day The Thinking Machine, through the window of his cell, spoke to the armed guard outside.

"What day of the month is it?" he asked.

"The fifteenth," was the answer.

The Thinking Machine made a mental astronomical calculation and satisfied himself that the moon would not rise until after nine o'clock that night. Then he asked another question:

"Who attends to those arc lights?"

"Man from the company."

"You have no electricians in the building?"

"No."

"I should think you could save money if you had your own man."

"None of my business," replied the guard.

The guard noticed The Thinking Machine at the cell window frequently during that day, but always the face seemed listless and there was a certain wistfulness in the squint eyes behind the glasses. After a while he accepted the presence of the leonine head as a matter of course. He had seen other prisoners do the same thing; it was the longing for the outside world.

That afternoon, just before the day guard was relieved, the head appeared at the window again, and The Thinking Machine's hand held something out between the bars. It fluttered to the ground and the guard picked it up. It was a five-dollar bill.

"That's for you," called the prisoner.

As usual, the guard took it to the warden. That gentleman looked at it suspiciously; he looked at every-thing that came from Cell 13 with suspicion.

"He said it was for me," explained the guard.

"It's a sort of a tip, I suppose," said the warden. "I see no particular reason why you shouldn't accept—"

Suddenly he stopped. He had remembered that The Thinking Machine had gone into Cell 13 with one five-dollar bill and two ten-dollar bills; twenty-five dol-lars in all. Now a five-dollar bill had been tied around the first piece of linen that came from the cell. The warden still had it, and to convince himself he took it out and looked at it. It was five dollars; yet here was another five dollars, and The Thinking Machine had only had ten dollar bills.

"Perhaps somebody changed one of the bills for him," he thought at last, with a sigh of relief.

But then and there he made up his mind. He would search Cell 13 as a cell was never before searched in this world. When a man could write at will, change money, and do other wholly inexplicable things, there was something radically wrong with his prison. He planned to enter the cell at night—three o'clock would be an excellent time. The Thinking Machine must do all the weird things he did some time. Night seemed the most reasonable.

Thus it happened that the warden stealthily de-scended upon Cell 13 that night at three o'clock. He paused at the door and listened. There was no sound save the steady, regular breathing of the prisoner. The keys unfastened the double locks with scarcely a clank, and the warden entered, locking the door behind him. Suddenly he flashed his dark-lantern in the face of the recumbent figure.

If the warden had planned to startle The Thinking Machine he was mistaken, for that individual merely opened his eyes quietly, reached for his glasses and inquired, in a most matter-of-fact tone:

"Who is it?"

It would be useless to describe the search that the warden made. It was minute. Not one inch of the cell or the bed was overlooked. He found the round hole in the floor, and with a flash of inspiration thrust his thick fingers into it. After a moment of fumbling there he drew up something and looked at it in the light of his lantern.

"Ugh!" he exclaimed.

The thing he had taken out was a rat—a dead rat. His inspiration fled as a mist before the sun. But he continued the search.

The Thinking Machine, without a word, rose and kicked the rat out of the cell into the corridor.

The warden climbed on the bed and tried the steel bars in the tiny window. They were perfectly rigid; every bar of the door was the same.

Then the warden searched the prisoner's clothing, beginning at the shoes. Nothing hidden in them! Then the trousers' waistband. Still nothing! Then the pockets of the trousers. From one side he drew out some paper money and examined it.

"Five one-dollar bills," he gasped.

"That's right," said the prisoner.

"But the—you had two tens and a five—what the—how do you do it?"

"That's my business," said The Thinking Machine.

"Did any of my men change this money for you—on your word of honor?"

The Thinking Machine paused just a fraction of a second.

"No," he said.

"Well, do you make it?" asked the warden. He was prepared to believe anything.

"That's my business," again said the prisoner.

The warden glared at the eminent scientist fiercely. He felt—he knew—that this man was making a fool of him, yet he didn't know how. If he were a real prisoner he would get the truth—but, then, perhaps, those inexplicable things which had happened would not have been brought before him so sharply. Neither of the men spoke for a long time, then suddenly the warden turned fiercely and left the cell, slamming the door behind him. He didn't dare to speak, then.

He glanced at the clock. It was ten minutes to four. He had hardly settled himself in bed when again came that heart-breaking shriek through the prison. With a few muttered words, which, while not elegant, were highly expressive, he relighted his lantern and rushed through the prison again to the cell on the upper floor.

Again Ballard was crushing himself against the steel

door, shrieking, shrieking at the top of his voice. He stopped only when the warden flashed his lamp in the cell.

"Take me out, take me out," he screamed. "I did it, I did it, I killed her. Take it away."

"Take what away?" asked the warden.

"I threw the acid in her face—I did it—I confess. Take me out of here."

Ballard's condition was pitiable; it was only an act of mercy to let him out into the corridor. There he crouched in a corner, like an animal at bay, and clasped his hands to his ears. It took half an hour to calm him sufficiently for him to speak. Then he told incoherently what had happened. On the night before at four o'clock he had heard a voice—a sepulchral voice, muffled and wailing in tone.

"What did it say?" asked the warden, curiously.

"Acid—acid—acid!" gasped the prisoner. "It accused me. Acid! I threw the acid, and the woman died. Oh!" It was a long, shuddering wail of terror.

"Acid?" echoed the warden, puzzled. The case was beyond him.

"Acid. That's all I heard—that one word, repeated several times. There were other things, too, but I didn't hear them."

"That was last night, eh?" asked the warden. "What happened to-night—what frightened you just now?"

"It was the same thing," gasped the prisoner. "Acid—acid—acid." He covered his face with his hands and sat shivering. "It was acid I used on her, but I didn't mean to kill her. I just heard the words. It was something accusing me—accusing me." He mumbled, and was silent.

"Did you hear anything else?"

"Yes—but I couldn't understand—only a little bit—just a word or two."

"Well, what was it?"

"I heard 'acid' three times, then I heard a long, moaning sound, then—then—I heard 'No. 8 hat.' I heard that voice."

"No. 8 hat," repeated the warden. "What the devil —No. 8 hat? Accusing voices of conscience have never talked about No. 8 hats, so far as I ever heard."

"He's insane," said one of the jailers, with an air of finality.

"I believe you," said the warden. "He must be. He probably heard something and got frightened. He's trembling now. No. 8 hat! What the—"

V

When the fifth day of The Thinking Machine's imprisonment rolled around the warden was wearing a haunted look. He was anxious for the end of the thing. He could not help but feel that his distinguished prisoner had been amusing himself. And if this were so, The Thinking Machine had lost none of his sense of humor. For on this fifth day he flung down another linen note to the outside guard, bearing the words: "Only two days more." Also he flung down half a dollar.

Now the warden knew—he *knew*—that the man in Cell 13 didn't have any half dollars—he *couldn't* have any half dollars, no more than he could have pen and ink, and yet he did have them. It was a condition, not a theory; that is one reason why the warden was wearing a haunted look.

That ghastly, uncanny thing, too, about "Acid" and "No. 8 hat" clung to him tenaciously. They didn't mean anything, of course, merely the ravings of an insane murderer who had been driven by fear to confess his crime, still there were so many things that "didn't mean anything" happening in the prison now since The Thinking Machine was there.

On the sixth day the warden received a postal stating that Dr. Ransome and Mr. Fielding would be at Chisholm Prison on the following evening, Thursday, and in the event Professor Van Dusen had not yet escaped—and they presumed he had not because they had not heard from him—they would meet him there.

"In the event he had not yet escaped!" The warden smiled grimly. Escaped!

The Thinking Machine enlivened this day for the warden with three notes. They were on the usual linen and bore generally on the appointment at half-past eight o'clock Thursday night, which appointment the scientist had made at the time of his imprisonment.

On the afternoon of the seventh day the warden

passed Cell 13 and glanced in. The Thinking Machine was lying on the iron bed, apparently sleeping lightly. The cell appeared precisely as it always did from a casual glance. The warden would swear that no man was going to leave it between that hour—it was then four o'clock—and half-past eight o'clock that evening.

On his way back past the cell the warden heard the steady breathing again, and coming close to the door looked in. He wouldn't have done so if The Thinking Machine had been looking, but now—well, it was different.

A ray of light came through the high window and fell on the face of the sleeping man. It occurred to the warden for the first time that his prisoner appeared haggard and weary. Just then The Thinking Machine stirred slightly and the warden hurried on up the corridor guiltily. That evening after six o'clock he saw the jailer.

"Everything all right in Cell 13?" he asked.

"Yes, sir," replied the jailer. "He didn't eat much, though."

It was with a feeling of having done his duty that the warden received Dr. Ransome and Mr. Fielding shortly after seven o'clock. He intended to show them the linen notes and lay before them the full story of his woes, which was a long one. But before this came to pass the guard from the river side of the prison yard entered the office.

"The arc light in my side of the yard won't light," he

informed the warden.

"Confound it, that man's a hoodoo," thundered the official. "Everything has happened since he's been here."

The guard went back to his post in the darkness, and the warden 'phoned to the electric light company.

"This is Chisholm Prison," he said through the 'phone. "Send three or four men down here quick, to fix an arc light."

The reply was evidently satisfactory, for the warden hung up the receiver and passed out into the yard. While Dr. Ransome and Mr. Fielding sat waiting, the guard at the outer gate came in with a special delivery letter. Dr. Ransome happened to notice the address, and, when the guard went out, looked at the letter more closely.

"By George!" he exclaimed.

"What is it?" asked Mr. Fielding.

Silently the doctor offered the letter. Mr. Fielding examined it closely.

"Coincidence," he said. "It must be."

It was nearly eight o'clock when the warden returned to his office. The electricians had arrived in a wagon, and were now at work. The warden pressed the buzz-button communicating with the man at the outer gate in the wall.

"How many electricians came in?" he asked, over the short 'phone. "Four? Three workmen in jumpers and overalls and the manager? Frock coat and silk hat? All right. Be certain that only four go out. That's all."

He turned to Dr. Ransome and Mr. Fielding. "We have to be careful here—particularly," and there was broad sarcasm in his tone, "since we have scientists locked up."

The warden picked up the special delivery letter carelessly, and then began to open it.

"When I read this I want to tell you gentlemen something about how—Great Caesar!" he ended, suddenly, as he glanced at the letter. He sat with mouth open, motionless, from astonishment.

"What is it?" asked Mr. Fielding.

"A special delivery letter from Cell 13," gasped the warden. "An invitation to supper."

"What?" and the two others arose, unanimously.

The warden sat dazed, staring at the letter for a moment, then called sharply to a guard outside in the corridor.

"Run down to Cell 13 and see if that man's in there."

The guard went as directed, while Dr. Ransome and Mr. Fielding examined the letter.

"It's Van Dusen's handwriting; there's no question of that," said Dr. Ransome. "I've seen too much of it."

Just then the buzz on the telephone from the outer gate sounded, and the warden, in a semi-trance, picked up the receiver.

"Hello! Two reporters, eh? Let 'em come in." He turned suddenly to the doctor and Mr. Fielding. "Why, the man *can't* be out. He must be in his cell."

Just at that moment the guard returned.

"He's still in his cell, sir," he reported. "I saw him. He's lying down."

"There, I told you so," said the warden, and he breathed freely again. "But how did he mail that letter?"

There was a rap on the steel door which led from the jail yard into the warden's office.

"It's the reporters," said the warden. "Let them in," he instructed the guard; then to the two other gentlemen: "Don't say anything about this before them, because I'd never hear the last of it."

The door opened, and the two men from the front gate entered.

"Good evening, gentlemen," said one. That was Hutchinson Hatch; the warden knew him well.

"Well?" demanded the other, irritably. "I'm here."

That was The Thinking Machine.

He squinted belligerently at the warden, who sat with mouth agape. For the moment that official had nothing to say. Dr. Ransome and Mr. Fielding were amazed, but they didn't know what the warden knew. They were only amazed; he was paralyzed. Hutchinson Hatch, the reporter, took in the scene with greedy eyes.

"How—how—how did you do it?" gasped the warden, finally.

"Come back to the cell," said The Thinking Machine, in the irritated voice which his scientific associates knew so well.

The warden, still in a condition bordering on trance, led the way.

"Flash your light in there," directed The Thinking Machine.

The warden did so. There was nothing unusual in the appearance of the cell, and there—there on the bed lay the figure of The Thinking Machine. Certainly! There was the yellow hair! Again the warden looked at the man beside him and wondered at the strangeness of his own dreams.

With trembling hands he unlocked the cell door and The Thinking Machine passed inside.

"See here," he said.

He kicked at the steel bars in the bottom of the cell door and three were pushed out of place. A fourth broke off and rolled away in the corridor.

"And here, too," directed the erstwhile prisoner as he stood on the bed to reach the small window. He swept his hand across the opening and every bar came out.

"What's this in the bed?" demanded the warden, who was slowly recovering.

"A wig," was the reply. "Turn down the cover."

The warden did so. Beneath it lay a large coil of strong rope, thirty feet or more, a dagger, three files, ten feet of electric wire, a thin, powerful pair of steel pliers, a small tack hammer with its handle, and—and a Derringer pistol.

"How did you do it?" demanded the warden.

"You gentlemen have an engagement to supper with me at half-past nine o'clock," said The Thinking Machine. "Come on, or we shall be late."

"But how did you do it?" insisted the warden.

"Don't ever think you can hold any man who can use his brain," said The Thinking Machine. "Come on; we shall be late."

VI

It was an impatient supper party in the rooms of Professor Van Dusen and a somewhat silent one. The guests were Dr. Ransome, Albert Fielding, the warden, and Hutchinson Hatch, reporter. The meal was served to the minute, in accordance with Professor Van Dusen's instructions of one week before; Dr. Ransome found the artichokes delicious. At last the supper was finished and The Thinking Machine turned full on Dr. Ransome and squinted at him fiercely.

"Do you believe it now?" he demanded.

"I do," replied Dr. Ransome.

"Do you admit that it was a fair test?"

"I do."

With the others, particularly the warden, he was waiting anxiously for the explanation.

"Suppose you tell us how—" began Mr. Fielding.

"Yes, tell us how," said the warden.

The Thinking Machine readjusted his glasses, took a couple of preparatory squints at his audience, and began the story. He told it from the beginning logically; and no man ever talked to more interested listeners.

"My agreement was," he began, "to go into a cell, carrying nothing except what was necessary to wear, and to leave that cell within a week. I had never seen Chisholm Prison. When I went into the cell I asked for tooth powder, two ten and one five-dollar bills, and also to have my shoes blacked. Even if these requests had been refused it would not have mattered seriously. But you agreed to them.

"I knew there would be nothing in the cell which you thought I might use to advantage. So when the warden locked the door on me I was apparently helpless, unless I could turn three seemingly innocent things to use. They were things which would have been permitted any prisoner under sentence of death, were they not, warden?"

"Tooth powder and polished shoes, yes, but not money," replied the warden.

"Anything is dangerous in the hands of a man who knows how to use it," went on The Thinking Machine. "I did nothing that first night but sleep and chase rats." He glared at the warden. "When the matter was broached I knew I could do nothing that night, so I suggested the next day. You gentlemen thought I wanted time to arrange an escape with outside assistance, but this was not true. I knew I could communicate with whom I pleased, when I pleased."

The warden stared at him a moment, then went on smoking solemnly.

"I was aroused next morning at six o'clock by the jailer with my breakfast," continued the scientist. "He told me dinner was at twelve and supper at six. Between these times, I gathered, I would be pretty much to myself. So immediately after breakfast I examined my outside surroundings from my cell window. One look told me it would be useless to try to scale the wall, even should I decide to leave my cell by the window, for my purpose was to leave not only the cell, but the prison. Of course, I could have gone over the wall, but it would have taken me longer to lay my plans that way. Therefore, for the moment, I dismissed all idea of that.

"From this first observation I knew the river was on that side of the prison, and that there was also a playground there. Subsequently these surmises were verified by a keeper. I knew then one important thing—that one might approach the prison wall from that side if necessary without attracting any particular attention. That was well to remember. I remembered it.

"But the outside thing which most attracted my attention was the feed wire to the arc light which ran within a few feet—probably three or four—of my cell window. I knew that would be valuable in the event I found it necessary to cut off that arc light."

"Oh, you shut it off to-night, then?" asked the warden.

"Having learned all I could from that window," resumed The Thinking Machine, without heeding the interruption, "I considered the idea of escaping through the cell, which I knew would be the only way. Seven doors lay between me and the outside. So, also for the time being, I gave up the idea of escaping that way. And I couldn't go through the solid granite walls of the cell."

The Thinking Machine paused for a moment and Dr. Ransome lighted a new cigar. For several minutes there was silence, then the scientific jail-breaker went on:

"While I was thinking about these things a rat ran across my foot. It suggested a new line of thought. There were at least half a dozen rats in the cell—I could see their beady eyes. Yet I had noticed none come under the cell door. I frightened them purposely and watched the cell door to see if they went out that way. They did not, but they were gone. Obviously they went another way. Another way meant another opening.

"I searched for this opening and found it. It was an old drain pipe, long unused and partly choked with dirt and dust. But this was the way the rats had come. They came from somewhere. Where? Drain pipes usually lead outside prison grounds. This one probably led to the river, or near it. The rats must therefore come from that direction. If they came a part of the way, I reasoned that they came all the way, because it was extremely unlikely that a solid iron or lead pipe would have any hole in it except at the exit.

"When the jailer came with my luncheon he told me two important things, although he didn't know it. One was that a new system of plumbing had been put in the prison seven years before; another that the river was only three hundred feet away. Then I knew positively that the pipe was a part of an old system; I knew, too, that it slanted generally toward the river. But did the pipe end in the water or on land?

"This was the next question to be decided. I decided it by catching several of the rats in the cell. My jailer was surprised to see me engaged in this work. I examined at least a dozen of them. They were perfectly dry; they had come through the pipe, and most important of all, they were *not house rats, but field rats*. The other end of the pipe was on land, then, outside the prison walls. So far, so good.

"Then, I knew that if I worked freely from this point I must attract the warden's attention in another direction. You see, by telling the warden that I had come there to escape you made the test more severe, because I had to trick him by false scents."

The warden looked up with a sad expression in his eyes.

"The first thing was to make him think I was trying to communicate with you, Dr. Ransome. So I wrote a note on a piece of linen I tore from my shirt, and addressed it to Dr. Ransome, tied a five-dollar bill around it and threw it out the window. I knew the guard would take it to the warden, but I rather hoped the warden would send it as addressed. Have you that first linen note, warden?"

The warden produced the cipher.

"What the deuce does it mean, anyhow?" he asked.

"Read it backward, beginning with the 'T' signature and disregard the division into words," instructed The Thinking Machine.

The warden did so.

"T-h-i-s, this," he spelled, studied it a moment, then read it off, grinning:

"This is not the way I intend to escape."

"Well, now what do you think o' that?" he demanded, still grinning.

"I knew that would attract your attention, just as it did," said The Thinking Machine, "and if you really found out what it was it would be a sort of gentle rebuke."

"What did you write it with?" asked Dr. Ransome, after he had examined the linen and passed it to Mr. Fielding.

"This," said the erstwhile prisoner, and he extended his foot. On it was the shoe he had worn in prison, though the polish was gone—scraped off clean. "The shoe blacking, moistened with water, was my ink; the metal tip of the shoe lace made a fairly good pen."

The warden looked up and suddenly burst into a laugh, half of relief, half of amusement.

"You're a wonder," he said, admiringly. "Go on."

"That precipitated a search of my cell by the warden, as I had intended," continued The Thinking Machine. "I was anxious to get the warden into the habit of searching my cell, so that finally, constantly finding nothing, he would get disgusted and quit. This at last happened, practically."

The warden blushed.

"He then took my white shirt away and gave me a prison shirt. He was satisfied that those two pieces of the shirt were all that was missing. But while he was searching my cell I had another piece of that same shirt, about nine inches square, rolled into a small ball in my mouth."

"Nine inches of that shirt?" demanded the warden. "Where did it come from?"

"The bosoms of all stiff white shirts are of triple thickness," was the explanation. "I tore out the inside thickness, leaving the bosom only two thicknesses. I knew you wouldn't see it. So much for that."

There was a little pause, and the warden looked from one to another of the men with a sheepish grin.

"Having disposed of the warden for the time being by giving him something else to think about, I took my first serious step toward freedom," said Professor Van Dusen. "I knew, within reason, that the pipe led somewhere to the playground outside; I knew a great many boys played there; I knew that rats came into my cell from out there. Could I communicate with someone outside with these things at hand?

"First was necessary, I saw, a long and fairly reliable thread, so—but here," he pulled up his trousers leg and showed that the tops of both stockings, of fine, strong lisle, were gone. "I unraveled those—after I got them started it wasn't difficult—and I had easily a quarter of a mile of thread that I could depend on.

"Then on half of my remaining linen I wrote, laboriously enough, I assure you, a letter explaining my situation to this gentleman here," and he indicated Hutchinson Hatch. "I knew he would assist me—for the value of the newspaper story. I tied firmly to this linen letter a ten-dollar bill—there is no surer way of attracting the eye of anyone—and wrote on the linen: 'Finder of this deliver to Hutchinson Hatch, *Daily American,* who will give another ten dollars for the information.'

"The next thing was to get this note outside on that playground where a boy might find it. There were two ways, but I chose the best. I took one of the rats—I became adept in catching them—tied the linen and money firmly to one leg, fastened my lisle thread to another, and turned him loose in the drain pipe. I reasoned that the natural fright of the rodent would make him run until he was outside the pipe and then out on earth he would probably stop to gnaw off the linen and money.

"From the moment the rat disappeared into that dusty pipe I became anxious. I was taking so many chances. The rat might gnaw the string, of which I held one end; other rats might gnaw it; the rat might run out of the pipe and leave the linen and money where they would never be found; a thousand other things might have happened. So began some nervous hours, but the fact that the rat ran on until only a few feet of the string remained in my cell made me think he was outside the pipe. I had carefully instructed Mr. Hatch what to do in case the note reached him. The question was: Would it reach him?

"This done, I could only wait and make other plans in case this one failed. I openly attempted to bribe my jailer, and learned from him that he held the keys to only two of seven doors between me and freedom. Then I did something else to make the warden nervous. I took the steel supports out of the heels of my shoes and made a pretense of sawing the bars of my cell window. The warden raised a pretty row about that. He developed, too, the habit of shaking the bars of my cell window to see if they were solid. They were —then."

Again the warden grinned. He had ceased being astonished.

"With this one plan I had done all I could and could only wait to see what happened," the scientist went on. "I couldn't know whether my note had been delivered or even found, or whether the rat had gnawed it up. And I didn't dare to draw back through the pipe that one slender thread which connected me with the outside.

"When I went to bed that night I didn't sleep, for fear there would come the slight twitch at the thread which was to tell me that Mr. Hatch had received the note. At half-past three o'clock, I judge, I felt this twitch, and no prisoner actually under sentence of death ever welcomed a thing more heartily."

The Thinking Machine stopped and turned to the reporter.

"You'd better explain just what you did," he said.

"The linen note was brought to me by a small boy who had been playing baseball," said Mr. Hatch. "I immediately saw a big story in it, so I gave the boy another ten dollars, and got several spools of silk, some twine, and a roll of light, pliable wire. The professor's note suggested that I have the finder of the note show me just where it was picked up, and told me to make my search from there, beginning at two o'clock in the morning. If I found the other end of the thread I was to twitch it gently three times, then a fourth.

"I began to search with a small pocket flashlight. It was an hour and twenty minutes before I found the end of the drain pipe, half hidden in weeds. The pipe was very large there, say twelve inches across. Then I found the end of the lisle thread, twitched it as directed and immediately I got an answering twitch.

"Then I fastened the silk to this and Professor Van Dusen began to pull it into his cell. I nearly had heart failure for fear the string would break. To the end of the silk I fastened the twine, and when that had been pulled in I tied on the wire. Then that was drawn into the pipe and we had a substantial line, which the rats couldn't gnaw, from the mouth of the drain into the cell."

The Thinking Machine raised his hand and Hatch stopped.

"All this was done in absolute silence," said the scientist. "But when the wire reached my hand I could have shouted. Then we tried another experiment, which Mr. Hatch was prepared for. I tested the pipe as a speaking tube. Neither of us could hear very clearly, but I dared not speak loud for fear of attracting attention in the prison. At last I made him understand what I wanted immediately. He seemed to have great difficulty in understanding when I asked for nitric acid, and I repeated the word 'acid' several times.

"Then I heard a shriek from a cell above me. I knew instantly that some one had overheard, and when I heard you coming, Mr. Warden, I feigned sleep. If you had entered my cell at that moment the whole plan of escape would have ended there. But you passed on. That was the nearest I ever came to being caught.

"Having established this improvised trolley it is easy to see how I got things in the cell and made them disappear at will. I merely dropped them back into the pipe. You, Mr. Warden, could not have reached the connecting wire with your fingers; they are too large. My fingers, you see, are longer and more slender. In addition I guarded the top of that pipe with a rat—you remember how."

"I remember," said the warden, with a grimace.

"I thought that if anyone were tempted to investigate that hole the rat would dampen his ardor. Mr. Hatch could not send me anything useful through the pipe until next night, although he did send me change for ten dollars as a test, so I proceeded with other parts of my plan. Then I evolved the method of escape, which I finally employed.

"In order to carry this out successfully it was necessary for the guard in the yard to get accustomed to seeing me at the cell window. I arranged this by dropping linen notes to him, boastful in tone, to make the warden believe, if possible, one of his assistants was communicating with the outside for me. I would stand at my window for hours gazing out, so the guard could see, and occasionally I spoke to him. In that way I learned that the prison had no electricians of its own, but was dependent upon the lighting company if anything should go wrong.

"That cleared the way to freedom perfectly. Early in the evening of the last day of my imprisonment, when it was dark, I planned to cut the feed wire which was only a few feet from my window, reaching it with an acid-tipped wire I had. That would make that side of the prison perfectly dark while the electricians were searching for the break. That would also bring Mr. Hatch into the prison yard.

"There was only one more thing to do before I actually began the work of setting myself free. This was to arrange final details with Mr. Hatch through our speaking tube. I did this within half an hour after the warden left my cell on the fourth night of my imprisonment. Mr. Hatch again had serious difficulty in understanding me, and I repeated the word 'acid' to him several times, and later the word: 'Number eight hat'—that's my size—and these were the things which made a prisoner upstairs confess to murder, so one of the jailers told me next day. This prisoner heard our voices, confused of course, through the pipe, which also went to his cell. The cell directly over me was not occupied, hence no one else heard.

"Of course the actual work of cutting the steel bars out of the window and door was comparatively easy with nitric acid, which I got through the pipe in thin bottles, but it took time. Hour after hour on the fifth and sixth and seventh days the guard below was looking at me as I worked on the bars of the window with the acid on a piece of wire. I used the tooth powder to prevent the acid spreading. I looked away abstractedly as I worked and each minute the acid cut deeper into the metal. I noted that the jailers always tried the door by shaking the upper part, never the lower bars, therefore I cut the lower bars, leaving them hanging in place by thin strips of metal. But that was a bit of dare-deviltry. I could not have gone that way so easily."

The Thinking Machine sat silent for several minutes.

"I think that makes everything clear," he went on. "Whatever points I have not explained were merely to confuse the warden and jailers. These things in my bed I brought in to please Mr. Hatch, who wanted to improve the story. Of course, the wig was necessary in my plan. The special delivery letter I wrote and directed in my cell with Mr. Hatch's fountain pen, then sent it out to him and he mailed it. That's all, I think."

"But your actually leaving the prison grounds and then coming in through the outer gate to my office?" asked the warden.

"Perfectly simple," said the scientist. "I cut the electric light wire with acid, as I said, when the current was off. Therefore when the current was turned on the arc didn't light. I knew it would take some time to find out what was the matter and make repairs. When the guard went to report to you the yard was dark, I crept out the window—it was a tight fit, too—replaced the bars by standing on a narrow ledge and remained in a shadow until the force of electricians arrived. Mr. Hatch was one of them.

"When I saw him I spoke and he handed me a cap, a jumper and overalls, which I put on within ten feet of you, Mr. Warden, while you were in the yard. Later Mr. Hatch called me, presumably as a workman, and together we went out the gate to get something out of the wagon. The gate guard let us pass out readily as two workmen who had just passed in. We changed our clothing and reappeared, asking to see you. We saw you. That's all."

There was silence for several minutes. Dr. Ransome was first to speak.

"Wonderful!" he exclaimed. "Perfectly amazing."

"How did Mr. Hatch happen to come with the electricians?" asked Mr. Fielding.

"His father is manager of the company," replied The Thinking Machine.

"But what if there had been no Mr. Hatch outside to help?"

"Every prisoner has one friend outside who would help him escape if he could."

"Suppose—just suppose—there had been no old plumbing system there?" asked the warden, curiously.

"There were two other ways out," said The Thinking Machine, enigmatically.

MAURICE LEBLANC

. . . born in France in 1864, started out as a hack journalist. Though he tried for many years to write fiction, he just couldn't make the grade.

One day he was asked by a magazine editor to write a short crime story—simply to fill up space. Without any particular idea in his head, Leblanc sat down and started to write, and from his pen, sprang the daring and gallant character of Arsène Lupin. In the earlier stories about this dashing young man, Arsène Lupin was a gentleman-burglar; but as Leblanc continued writing about him, Lupin was changed from a thief to a detective.

In "Shadowed by Death," Arsène Lupin shows remarkable powers of deduction in the best detective tradition. As he goes about his business of tracking down the cold-blooded killer, the reader experiences a growing feeling of confidence—well-mixed with mounting suspense—that the case is in the best possible hands.

A beautiful girl

SHADOWED BY DEATH

harbors a killer under her roof

AFTER he had been round the walls of the property, Arsène Lupin returned to the spot from which he started. It was perfectly clear to him that there was no breach in the walls; and the only way of entering the extensive grounds of the Château de Maupertuis was through a little low door, firmly bolted on the inside, or through the principal gate, which was overlooked by the lodge.

"Very well," he said. "We must employ heroic methods."

Pushing his way into the copsewood where he had hidden his motorcycle, Lupin unwound a length of twine from under the saddle and went to a place which he had noticed in the course of his exploration. At this place, which was situated far from the road, on the edge of a wood, a number of large trees, standing inside the park, overlapped the wall.

Lupin fastened a stone to the string, threw it up and caught a thick branch, which he drew down to him and bestraddled. The branch, in recovering its position, raised him from the ground. He climbed over the wall, slipped down the tree, and sprang lightly on the grass.

It was winter; and, through the leafless boughs, across the undulating lawns, he could see the little Château de Maupertuis in the distance. Fearing lest he should be perceived, he concealed himself behind a clump of fir trees. From there, with the aid of a field glass, he studied the dark and melancholy front of the manor house. All the windows were closed and, as it were, barricaded with solid shutters. The house might easily have been uninhabited.

"Sapristi!" muttered Lupin. "It's not the liveliest of residences. I shall certainly not come here to end my days!"

But the clock struck three, one of the doors on the ground floor opened; and the figure of a woman appeared, a very slender figure wrapped in a brown cloak.

The woman walked up and down for a few minutes and was at once surrounded by birds, to which she scattered crumbs of bread. Then she went down the stone steps that led to the middle lawn and skirted it, taking the path on the right.

With his field glass, Lupin could distinctly see her

coming in his direction. She was tall, fair-haired, graceful in appearance, and seemed to be quite a young girl. She walked with a sprightly step, looking at the pale December sun and amusing herself by breaking the little dead twigs on the shrubs along the road.

She had gone nearly two thirds of the distance that separated her from Lupin when there came a furious sound of fierce barking and a huge dog, a colossal great Dane, sprang from a neighboring kennel and stood erect at the end of the chain by which it was fastened.

The girl moved a little to one side, without paying further attention to what was doubtless a daily incident. The dog grew angrier than ever, standing on its hind legs and dragging at its collar, at the risk of strangling itself.

Thirty or forty steps further, yielding probably to an impulse of impatience, the girl turned round and made a gesture with her hand. The great Dane gave a start of rage, retreated to the back of its kennel and rushed out again, this time unfettered. The girl uttered a cry of mad terror. The dog was covering the space between them, trailing its broken chain behind it.

She began to run, to run with all her might, and screamed out desperately for help. But the dog came up with her in a few bounds.

She fell, at once exhausted, giving herself up for lost. The animal was already upon her, almost touching her.

At that exact moment a shot rang out. The dog turned a complete somersault, recovered its feet, tore

the ground and then lay down, giving a number of
hoarse, breathless howls, which ended in a dull moan
and an indistinct gurgling. And that was all.

"Dead," said Lupin, who had hastened up at once,
prepared, if necessary, to fire his revolver a second time.

The girl had risen and stood pale, still staggering.
She looked in great surprise at this man whom she did
not know and who had saved her life; and she whispered:

"Thank you . . . I have had a great fright . . . You
were in the nick of time. . . . I thank you, monsieur."

Lupin took off his hat:

"Allow me to introduce myself, mademoiselle. . . .
My name is Paul Daubreuil. . . . But before entering
into any explanations, I must ask for one moment. . . ."

He stooped over the dog's dead body and examined
the chain at the part where the brute's effort had
snapped it:

"That's it," he said, between his teeth. "It's just as
I suspected. Parbleu, but things are moving rapidly! . . .
I ought to have come earlier."

Returning to the girl's side, he said to her, speaking
very quickly:

"Mademoiselle, we have not a minute to lose. My
presence in these grounds is quite irregular. I do not
wish to be surprised here; and this for reasons that concern yourself alone. Do you think that the shot can
have been heard at the house?"

The girl seemed already to have recovered from her
emotion; and she replied, with calmness that revealed

all her pluck:

"I don't think so."

"Is your father in the house to-day?"

"My father is ill and has been in bed for months. Besides, his room looks out on the other front."

"And the servants?"

"Their quarters and the kitchen are also on the other side. No one ever comes to this part. I walk here my-self, but nobody else does."

"It is probable, therefore, that I have not been seen either, especially as the trees hide us?"

"It is most probable."

"Then I can speak to you freely?"

"Certainly, but I don't understand. . . ."

"You will, presently. Permit me to be brief. The point is this: four days ago, Mlle. Jeanne Darcieux . . ."

"That is my name," she said, smiling.

"Mlle. Jeanne Darcieux," continued Lupin, "wrote a letter to one of her friends, called Marceline, who lives at Versailles. . . ."

"How do you know all that?" asked the girl, in astonishment. "I tore up the letter before I had finished it."

"And you flung the pieces on the edge of the road that runs from the house to Vendôme."

"That's true. . . . I had gone out walking. . . ."

"The pieces were picked up and they came into my hands next day."

"Then . . . you must have read them," said Jeanne Darcieux, betraying a certain annoyance by her manner. She looked at him, up and down.

"Yes, I committed that indiscretion; and I do not regret it, because I can save you."

"Save me? From what?"

"From death."

Lupin spoke this little sentence in a very distinct voice. The girl gave a shudder. Then she said:

"I am not threatened with death."

"Yes, you are, mademoiselle. At the end of October, you were reading on a bench on the terrace where you were accustomed to sit at the same hour every day, when a block of stone fell from the cornice above your head and you were within a few inches of being crushed."

"An accident. . . ."

"One fine evening in November, you were walking in the kitchen garden, by moonlight. A shot was fired. The bullet whizzed past your ear."

"At least, I thought so."

"Lastly, less than a week ago, the little wooden bridge that crosses the river in the park, two yards from the waterfall, gave way while you were on it. You were just able, by a miracle, to catch hold of the root of a tree."

Jeanne Darcieux tried to smile.

"Very well. But, as I wrote Marceline, these are only a series of coincidences, of accidents. . . ."

"No, mademoiselle, no. One accident of this sort is allowable. . . . So are two . . . and even then! . . . But we have no right to suppose that the chapter of accidents, repeating the same act three times in such different and extraordinary circumstances, is a mere amusing coincidence. That is why I thought that I might presume to come to your assistance. And, as my intervention can be of no use unless it remains secret, I did not hesitate to make my way in here . . . without walking through the gate. I came in the nick of time, as you said. Your enemy was attacking you once more."

"What! . . . Do you think? . . . No, it is impossible . . . I refuse to believe . . ."

Lupin picked up the chain and, showing it to her:

"Look at the last link. There is no question but that it has been filed. Otherwise, so powerful a chain as this would never have yielded. Besides, you can see the mark of the file here."

Jeanne turned pale and her pretty features were distorted with terror:

"But who can bear me such a grudge?" she gasped. "It is terrible. . . . I have never done any one harm. . . . And yet you are certainly right. . . . Worse still . . ."

She finished her sentence in a lower voice:

"Worse still, I am wondering whether the same danger does not threaten my father."

"Has he been attacked also?"

"No, for he never stirs from his room. But his is such a mysterious illness! . . . He has no strength . . . he cannot walk at all. . . . In addition to that, he is subject to fits of suffocation, as though his heart stopped beating. . . . Oh, what an awful thing!"

Lupin mustered all the authority which he was able

to assert at such a moment, and he said:

"Have no fear, mademoiselle. If you obey me blind-
ly, I shall be sure to succeed."

"Yes . . . yes . . . I am quite willing . . . but all this
is so terrible. . . ."

"Trust me, I beg of you. And please listen to me, I
shall want a few particulars."

He rapped out a number of questions, which Jeanne
Darcieux answered hurriedly:

"That animal was never let loose, was he?"

"Never."

"Who used to feed him?"

"The lodge-keeper. He brought him his food every
evening."

"Consequently, he could go near him without being
bitten?"

"Yes; and he only, for the dog was very savage."

"You don't suspect the man?"

"Oh, no! . . . Baptiste? . . . Never!"

"And you can't think of anybody?"

"No. Our servants are quite devoted to us. They
are very fond of me."

"You have no friends staying in the house?"

"No."

"No brother?"

"No."

"Then your father is your only protector?"

"Yes; and I have told you the condition he is in."

"Have you told him of the different attempts?"

"Yes; and it was wrong of me to do so. Our doctor,

old Dr. Guéroult, forbade me to cause him the least excitement."

"Your mother? . . ."

"I don't remember her. She died sixteen years ago . . . just sixteen years ago."

"How old were you then?"

"I was not quite five years old."

"And were you living here?"

"We were living in Paris. My father only bought this place the year after."

Lupin was silent for a few moments. Then he concluded:

"Very well, mademoiselle, I am obliged to you. Those particulars are all I need for the present. Besides, it would not be wise for us to remain together longer."

"But," she said, "the lodge-keeper will find the dog soon. . . . Who will have killed him?"

"You, mademoiselle, to defend yourself against an attack."

"I never carry firearms."

"I am afraid you do," said Lupin, smiling, "because you killed the dog and there is no one but you who could have killed him. For that matter, let them think what they please. The important thing is that I shall not be suspected when I come to the house."

"To the house? Do you intend to?"

"Yes. I don't yet know how . . . But I shall come . . . This very evening. . . . So, once more, be easy in your mind. I will answer for everything."

Jeanne looked at him and, dominated by him, conquered by his air of assurance and good faith, she said, simply:

"My mind is at ease."

"Then all will go well. Till this evening, mademoiselle."

"Till this evening."

She walked away; and Lupin, following her with his eyes until the moment when she disappeared round the corner of the house, murmured:

"What a pretty creature! It would be a pity if any harm were to come to her. Luckily, Arsène Lupin is keeping his weather eye open."

Taking care not to be seen, with eyes and ears attentive to the least sight or sound, he inspected every nook and corner of the grounds, looked for the little low door which he had noticed outside and which was the door of the kitchen garden, drew the bolt, took the key and then skirted the walls and found himself once more near the tree which he had climbed. Two minutes later, he was mounting his motorcycle.

*   *   *

The village of Maupertuis lay quite close to the estate. Lupin inquired and learned that Dr. Guéroult lived next door to the church.

He rang, was shown into the consulting-room and introduced himself by his name of Paul Daubreuil, of the Rue de Surène, Paris, adding that he had official relations with the detective service, a fact which he requested might be kept secret. He had become acquainted, by means of a torn letter, with the incidents that had endangered Mlle. Darcieux's life; and he had come to that young lady's assistance.

Dr. Guéroult, an old country practitioner, who idolized Jeanne, on hearing Lupin's explanations at once admitted that those incidents constituted undeniable proofs of a plot. He showed great concern, offered his visitor hospitality and kept him to dinner.

The two men talked at length. In the evening, they walked round to the manor house together.

The doctor went to the sick man's room, which was on the first floor, and asked leave to bring up a young colleague, to whom he intended soon to make over his practice, when he retired.

Lupin, on entering, saw Jeanne Darcieux seated by her father's bedside. She suppressed a movement of surprise and, at a sign from the doctor, left the room.

The consultation thereupon took place in Lupin's presence. M. Darcieux's face was worn with much suffering and his eyes were bright with fever. He complained particularly, that day, of his heart. After the auscultation, he questioned the doctor with obvious anxiety; and each reply seemed to give him relief. He also spoke of Jeanne and expressed his conviction that they were deceiving him and that his daughter had escaped yet more accidents. He continued, perturbed, in spite of the doctor's denials. He wanted to have the police informed and inquiries set afoot.

But his excitement tired him and he gradually dropped off to sleep.

Lupin stopped the doctor in the passage:

"Come, doctor, give me your exact opinion. Do you think that M. Darcieux's illness can be attributed to an outside cause?"

"How do you mean?"

"Well, suppose that the same enemy should be interested in removing both father and daughter."

The doctor seemed struck by the suggestion.

"Upon my word, there is something in what you say. . . . The father's illness at times adopts such a very unusual character! . . . For instance, the paralysis of the legs, which is almost complete, ought to be accompanied by . . ."

The doctor reflected for a moment and then said in a low voice:

"You think it's poison, of course . . . but what poison? . . . Besides, I see no toxic symptoms. . . . It would have to be . . . But what are you doing? What's the matter? . . ."

The two men were talking outside a little sitting-room on the first floor, where Jeanne, seizing the opportunity while the doctor was with her father, had begun her evening meal. Lupin, who was watching her through the open door, saw her lift a cup to her lips and take a few sips.

Suddenly, he rushed at her and caught her by the arm:

"What are you drinking there?"

"Why," she said, taken aback, "only tea!"

"You made a grimace of disgust . . . what caused you to do that?"

"I don't know . . . I thought . . ."

"You thought what?"

"That . . . that it tasted rather bitter. . . . But I expect that comes from the medicine I mixed with it."

"What medicine?"

"Some drops which I take at dinner . . . the drops which you prescribed for me, you know, doctor."

"Yes," said Dr. Guéroult, "but that medicine has no taste of any kind. . . . You know it hasn't, Jeanne, for you have been taking it for a fortnight and this is the first time . . ."

"That's right," said the girl, "and this does have a taste. . . . There—oh!—my mouth is still burning."

Dr. Guéroult now took a sip from the cup. "Faugh!" he exclaimed, spitting it out again. "There's no mistake about it. . . ."

Lupin, for his part, was examining the bottle containing the medicine; and he asked:

"Where is this bottle kept in the daytime?"

But Jeanne was unable to answer. She had put her hand to her heart and, wan-faced, with staring eyes, seemed to be suffering great pain:

"It hurts . . . it hurts," she stammered.

The two men quickly carried her to her room and laid her on the bed:

"She ought to have an emetic," said Lupin.

"Open the cupboard," said the doctor. "You'll see a medicine case. . . . Have you got it? . . . Take out one of those little tubes. . . . Yes, that one. . . . And now some hot water. . . . You'll find some on the tea tray in the other room." He pointed to where it was.

Jeanne's own maid came running up in answer to the bell. Lupin told her that Mlle. Darcieux had been taken ill, for some unknown reason.

He next returned to the little dining room, inspected the sideboard and the cupboards, went down to the kitchen and pretended that the doctor had sent him to ask about M. Darcieux's diet. Without appearing to do so, he catechized the cook, the butler, and Baptiste, the lodge-keeper, who had his meals at the manor house with the servants. Then he went back to the doctor:

"She's asleep."

"Any danger?"

"No. Fortunately, she had only taken two or three sips. But this is the second time to-day that you saved her life, as the analysis of this bottle will show."

"Quite superfluous to make an analysis, doctor. There is no doubt about the fact that there has been an attempt at poisoning."

"By whom?"

"I can't say. But the demon who is engineering all this business clearly knows the ways of the house. He comes and goes as he pleases, walks about in the park, files the dog's chain, mixes poison with the food and, in short, moves and acts precisely as though he were living the very life of her—or rather of those—whom he wants to put away."

"Ah! You really believe that M. Darcieux is threatened with the same danger?"

"I haven't the slightest doubt about it."

"Then it must be one of the servants? But that is most unlikely! Do you think . . .?"

"I think nothing, doctor. I know nothing. All I can say is that the situation is most tragic and that we must be prepared for the worst. Death is here, doctor, shadowing the people in this house; and it will soon strike at those whom it is pursuing."

"What's to be done?"

"Watch, doctor. Let us pretend that we are alarmed about M. Darcieux's health and spend the night here. The bedrooms of both father and daughter are close by. If anything happens, we are sure to hear."

There was an easy chair in the room. They arranged to take turns sleeping in it.

In reality, Lupin slept for only two or three hours. In the middle of the night he left the room, without disturbing his companion, carefully looked round the house and walked out through the main gate.

*   *   *

He reached Paris on his motorcycle at nine o'clock in the morning. Two of his friends, to whom he telephoned on the road, met him there. They all three spent the day in making searches which Lupin had planned out beforehand.

He set out again hurriedly at six o'clock; and never, perhaps, as he told me subsequently, did he risk his life with greater temerity than in his breakneck ride, at a mad rate of speed, on a foggy December evening, with the light of his lamp hardly able to pierce through the darkness. But speed was essential.

He sprang from his machine outside the gate, which was still open, ran to the house and reached the first floor in a few bounds.

There was no one in the little dining room.

Without hesitating, without knocking, he walked into Jeanne's bedroom:

"Ah, here you are!" he said, with a sigh of relief, seeing Jeanne and the doctor sitting side by side, talking.

"What? Any news?" asked the doctor, alarmed at seeing such a state of agitation in a man whose coolness he had had occasion to observe.

"No," said Lupin. "No news. And here?"

"None here, either. We have just left M. Darcieux. He has had an excellent day and he ate his dinner with a good appetite. As for Jeanne, you can see for yourself, she has all her pretty color back again."

"Then she must go."

"Go? But it's out of the question!" protested the girl.

"You must go, you must!" cried Lupin, with real violence.

He at once mastered himself, spoke a few words of apology and then, for three or four minutes, preserved a complete silence, which the doctor and Jeanne were careful not to disturb.

At last, he said to the young girl:

"You shall go to-morrow morning, mademoiselle. It will be only for one or two weeks. I will take you to your friend at Versailles, the one to whom you were writing. I entreat you to get everything ready to-night . . . without concealment of any kind. Let the servants know that you are going. . . . On the other hand, the doctor will be good enough to tell M. Darcieux and give him to understand, with every possible precaution, that this journey is essential to your safety. Besides, he can join you as soon as his strength permits. . . . That's settled, is it not?''

"Yes," she said, absolutely dominated by Lupin's gentle and imperious voice.

"In that case," he said, "be as quick as you can . . . and do not stir from your room. . . .''

"But," said the girl, with a shudder, "am I to stay alone to-night?''

"Fear nothing. Should there be the least danger, the doctor and I will come back. Do not open your door unless you hear three very light taps.''

Jeanne at once rang for her maid. The doctor went to M. Darcieux, while Lupin had some supper brought to him in the little dining-room.

"That's done," said the doctor, returning to him in twenty minutes' time. "M. Darcieux did not raise any great difficulty. As a matter of fact, he himself thinks it just as well we should send Jeanne away.''

They then went downstairs together and left the house.

On reaching the lodge, Lupin called the keeper.

"You can shut the gate, my man. If M. Darcieux should want us, send for us at once.''

The clock of Maupertuis church struck ten. The sky was overcast with black clouds, through which the moon broke at moments.

The two men walked on for sixty or seventy yards. They were nearing the village, when Lupin gripped his companion by the arm:

"Stop!"

"What on earth's the matter?" exclaimed the doctor.

"The matter is this," Lupin jerked out, "that, if my calculations turn out right, if I have not misjudged the business from start to finish, Mlle. Darcieux will be murdered before the night is out."

"Eh? What's that?" gasped the doctor, in dismay. "But then why did we go?"

"With the precise object that the miscreant, who is watching all our movements in the dark, may not postpone his crime and may perpetrate it, not at the hour chosen by himself, but at the hour which I have decided upon."

"Then we are returning to the manor house?"

"Yes, of course we are, but separately."

"In that case, let us go at once."

"Listen to me, doctor," said Lupin, in a steady voice, "and let us waste no time in useless words. Above all, we must defeat any attempt to watch us. You will therefore go straight home and not come out again until you are certain that you have not been followed. You will then make for the walls of the property, keeping to the left, till you come to the little door of the kitchen garden. Here is the key. When the church clock strikes eleven, open the door very gently and walk right up to the terrace at the back of the house. The fifth window is badly fastened. You have only to climb over the balcony. As soon as you are inside Mlle. Darcieux's room, bolt the door and don't budge. You quite understand, don't budge, either of you, whatever happens. I have noticed that Mlle. Darcieux leaves her dressing-room window ajar, isn't that so?"

"Yes, it's a habit which I taught her."

"That's the way they'll come."

"And you?"

"That's the way I shall come also."

"And do you know who the villain is?"

Lupin hesitated and then replied:

"No, I don't know. . . . And that is just how we shall find out. But, I implore you, keep cool. Not a word, not a movement, *whatever happens!*"

"I promise you."

"I want more than that, doctor. You must give me your word of honor."

"I give you my word of honor."

The doctor went away. Lupin at once climbed a neighboring hill, from which he could easily see the windows of the first and second floor. Several of them were lighted.

He waited for some little time. The lights went out one by one. Then, taking a direction opposite to that in which the doctor had gone, he branched off to the right and skirted the wall until he came to the clump of trees near which he had hidden his motorcycle on the day before. He impatiently waited his time.

Eleven o'clock struck. He calculated the time which it would take the doctor to cross the kitchen garden and make his way into the house.

"That's one point scored!" he muttered. "Everything's all right on that side. And now, Lupin to the rescue! The enemy won't be long before he plays his last trump . . . and, by all the gods, I must be there! . . ."

He went through the same performance as on the first occasion, pulled down the branch and hoisted himself to the top of the wall, from which he was able to reach the bigger boughs of the tree.

Just then he pricked up his ears. He seemed to hear a rustling of dead leaves. And he actually perceived a dark form moving on the level thirty yards away:

"Hang it all!" he said to himself. "I'm done: the scoundrel has smelt a rat."

A moonbeam pierced through the clouds. Lupin distinctly saw the man take aim. He tried to jump to the ground and turned his head. But he felt something hit him in the chest, heard the sound of a report, uttered an angry oath and came crashing down from branch to branch, like a corpse.

*   *   *

Meanwhile, Doctor Guéroult, following Arsène Lupin's instructions, had climbed the ledge of the fifth window and groped his way to the second floor. On reaching Jeanne's room, he tapped lightly, three times, at the door and, immediately on entering, pushed the bolt. His voice was frought with tenseness.

"Lie down at once," he whispered to the girl, who had not taken off her things. "You must appear to have gone to bed. Brrr, it's cold in here! Is the window open in your dressing-room?"

"Yes . . . would you like me to . . .?"

"No, leave it as it is. They are coming."

"They are coming!" spluttered Jeanne, in affright.

"Yes, beyond a doubt."

"But who? Do you suspect any one?"

"I don't know who . . . I expect that there is some one hidden in the house . . . or in the park."

"Oh, I feel so frightened!"

"Don't be frightened. The sportsman who's looking after you seems very clever and makes a point of playing a safe game. I expect he's on the lookout in the court."

The doctor put out the night-light, went to the window and raised the blind. A narrow cornice, running along the second story, kept him from seeing more than a distant part of the courtyard; and he came back and sat down by the bed.

Some very painful minutes passed, minutes that appeared to them interminably long. The clock in the village struck; but, taken up as they were with all the little noises of the night, they hardly noticed the sound. They listened, listened, with all their nerves on edge:

"Did you hear?" whispered the doctor.

"Yes . . . yes," said Jeanne sitting up in bed.

"Lie down . . . lie down," he said, presently. "There's

some one coming," he said in a whisper.

There was a little tapping sound outside, against the cornice. Next came a series of indistinct noises, the nature of which they could not make out for certain. But they had a feeling that the window in the dressing room was being opened wider, for they were buffeted by gusts of cold air.

Suddenly, it became quite clear: there was some one next door.

The doctor, whose hand was trembling a little, seized his revolver. Nevertheless, he did not move, remembering the formal orders which he had received and fearing to act against them.

The room was in absolute darkness; and they were unable to see where the adversary was. But they felt his presence.

They followed his invisible movements, the sound of his footsteps deadened by the carpet; and they did not doubt that he had already crossed the threshold of the room.

And the adversary stopped. Of that they were certain. He was standing six steps away from the bed, motionless, undecided perhaps, seeking to pierce the darkness with his keen eyes.

Jeanne's hand, icy-cold and clammy, trembled in the doctor's grasp.

With his other hand, the doctor clutched his revolver, with his finger on the trigger. In spite of his pledged word, he did not hesitate. If the adversary touched the end of the bed, the shot would be fired at will. There was nothing else he could do.

The adversary took another step and then stopped again. And there was something awful about that silence, that impassive silence, that darkness in which those human beings were peering at one another, wildly.

Who was it looming in the murky darkness? Who was the man? What horrible enmity was it that turned his hand against the girl and what abominable aim was he pursuing?

Terrified though they were, Jeanne and the doctor thought only of that one thing: to see, to learn the truth, to gaze upon the adversary's face.

He took one more step and halted once again. It seemed to them that his figure stood out, darker, against the dark space and that his arm rose slowly, slowly . . .

A minute passed and then another minute . . .

And, suddenly, beyond the man, on the right a sharp click. . . . A bright light flashed, was flung upon the man, hit him full in the face, remorselessly.

Jeanne gave a cry of affright. She had seen—standing over her, with a dagger in his hand—she had seen . . . *her father!*

Almost at the same time, though the light was already turned off, there came a report: the doctor had fired.

"Dash it all, don't shoot!" roared Lupin.

He threw his arms round the doctor, who choked out:

"Didn't you see? . . . Listen! . . . He's escaping! . . . "

"Let him: it's the best thing that could happen."

He pressed the switch of his electric lantern again, ran to the dressing-room, made certain that the man had disappeared and, returning quietly to the table, lit the lamp.

Jeanne lay on her bed, pallid, in a dead faint.

The doctor, huddled in his chair, emitted inarticulate sounds.

"Come," said Lupin, laughing, "pull yourself together. There is nothing to excite ourselves about: it's all over."

"Her father! . . . Her father!" moaned the old doctor.

"If you please, doctor, Mlle. Darcieux is ill. Look after her."

Without more words, Lupin went back to the dressing-room and stepped out on the window ledge. A ladder stood against the ledge. He ran down it. Skirting the wall of the house, twenty steps farther, he tripped over the rungs of a rope ladder, which he climbed and found himself in M. Darcieux's bedroom. The room was empty.

"Just so," he said. "My gentleman did not like the position and has cleared out. Here's wishing him a good journey. . . . And, of course, the door is bolted? . . . Exactly! . . . That is how our sick man, tricking his worthy medical attendant, used to get up at night in full security, fasten his rope ladder to the balcony and prepare his little games. He's no fool, is friend

Darcieux!"

He drew the bolts and returned to Jeanne's room. The doctor, who was just coming out of the doorway, drew him to the little dining-room:

"She's asleep, don't let us disturb her. She has had a bad shock and will take some time to recover."

Lupin poured out a glass of water for himself and drank it down. Then he took a chair and said, calmly:

"Pooh! She'll be all right by to-morrow."

"What do you say?"

"I say that she'll be all right by tomorrow."

"Why?"

"In the first place, because it did not strike me that Mlle. Darcieux felt any very great affection for her father."

"Never mind! Think of it: a father who tries to kill his daughter! A father who, for months on end, repeats his monstrous attempt four, five, six times over again! . . . Well, isn't that enough to blight a less sensitive soul than Jeanne's for good and all? What a hateful memory!"

"She will forget."

"One does not forget such a thing as that."

"She will forget, doctor, and for a very simple reason. . . ."

"Explain yourself!"

"She is not M. Darcieux's daughter!"

"Eh?"

"I repeat, she is not that villain's daughter."

"What do you mean? M. Darcieux . . . "

"M. Darcieux is only her stepfather. She had just been born when her father, her real father, died. Jeanne's mother than married a cousin of her husband's, a man bearing the same name, and she died within a year of her second wedding. She left Jeanne in M. Darcieux's charge. He first took her abroad and then bought this country house; and, as nobody knew him in the neighborhood, he represented the child as being his daughter. She herself did not know the truth about her birth."

The doctor sat confounded. He asked:

"Are you sure of your facts?"

"I spent my day in the town halls of the Paris municipalities. I searched the registers, I interviewed two solicitors, I have seen all the documents. There is no doubt possible."

"But that does not explain the crime, or rather the series of crimes."

"Yes, it does," declared Lupin. "And, from the start, from the first hour when I meddled in this business, some words which Mlle. Darcieux used made me suspect that direction which my investigations must take. 'I was not quite five years old when my mother died,' she said. 'That was sixteen years ago.' Mlle. Darcieux, therefore, was nearly twenty-one, that is to say, she was on the verge of attaining her majority. I at once saw that this was an important detail. The day on which you reach your majority is the day on which your accounts are rendered. What was the financial position of Mlle. Darcieux, who was her mother's natural heiress? Of course, I did not think of her father for a second. To begin with, one can't imagine a thing like that; and then the farce which M. Darcieux was playing . . . helpless, bedridden, ill . . . "

"Really ill," interrupted the doctor.

"All this diverted suspicion from him . . . the more so as I believed that he himself was exposed to criminal attacks. But was there not in the family some person who would be interested in their removal? My journey to Paris revealed the truth to me: Mlle. Darcieux inherits a large fortune from her mother, of which her stepfather draws the income. The solicitor was to have called a meeting of the family in Paris next month. The truth would have been out. It meant ruin to M. Darcieux."

"Then he had put no money by?"

"Yes, but he had lost a great deal as the result of unfortunate speculations."

"But, after all, Jeanne would not have taken the management of her fortune out of his hands!"

"There is one detail which you do not know, doctor, and which I learned from reading the torn letter. Mlle. Darcieux is in love with the brother of Marceline, her Versailles friend; M. Darcieux was opposed to the marriage; and—you now see the reason—she was waiting until she came of age to be married."

"You're right," said the doctor, "you're right. . . . It meant his ruin."

"His absolute ruin. One chance of saving himself remained, the death of his stepdaughter, of whom he is the next heir."

"Certainly, but on condition that no one suspected him," interrupted the doctor.

"Of course; and that is why he contrived the series of accidents, so that the death might appear to be due to misadventure. And that is why I, on my side, wishing to bring things to a head, asked you to tell him of Mlle. Darcieux's impending departure. From that moment, it was no longer enough for the would-be sick man to wander about the grounds and the passages, in the dark, and execute some leisurely thought-out plan. No, he had to act, to act at once, without preparation, violently, dagger in hand. I had no doubt that he would decide to do it. And he did."

"Then he had no suspicions?"

"Of me, yes. He felt that I would return tonight, and he kept a watch at the place where I had already climbed the wall."

"Well?"

"Well," said Lupin, laughing, "I received a bullet full in the chest . . . or, rather, my wallet received a bullet. . . . Here, you can see the hole. . . . So I tumbled from the tree, like a dead man. Thinking that he was rid of his only adversary, he went back to the house. I saw him prowl about for two hours. Then, making up his mind, he went to the coach house, took a ladder and set it against the window. I had only to follow him."

The doctor reflected and said:

"You could have collared him earlier. Why did you

let him come up? It was a sore trial for Jeanne . . . and unnecessary."

"On the contrary, it was indispensable! Mlle. Darcieux would never have accepted the truth. It was essential that she should see the murderer's very face. You must tell her all the circumstances when she wakes. She will soon be well again."

"But . . . M. Darcieux?"

"You can explain his disappearance as you think best . . . a sudden journey . . . a fit of madness. . . . There will be a few inquiries. . . . And you may be sure that he will never be heard of again."

The doctor nodded his head:

"Yes . . . that is so . . . that is so . . . you are right. You have managed all this business with extraordinary skill; and Jeanne owes you her life. She will thank you in person. . . . But now, can I be of use to you in any way? You told me that you were connected with the detective-service. . . . Will you allow me to write and praise your conduct, your courage?"

Lupin began to laugh:

"Certainly! A letter of that kind will do me a world of good. You might write to my immediate superior, Chief-Inspector Ganimard. He will be glad to hear that his favorite officer, Paul Daubreuil, of the Rue de Surène, has once again distinguished himself by a brilliant action. As it happens, I have an appointment to meet him about a case of which you may have heard: the case of the red scarf . . . How pleased my dear M. Ganimard will be!"

GILBERT KEITH CHESTERTON
(1874-1936)

. . . combined a brilliant wit with an independent mind that led him to espouse some of the most controversial opinions of his day. While George Bernard Shaw and other of his contemporaries advocated Socialism, Chesterton vigorously rejected it, offering instead his own theory of Distributism. Furthermore, in Anglican England, Chesterton was a dogged and militant Catholic.

Physically, the man was enormous. His dishevelled hair and mustache, and thin-rimmed spectacles perched precariously on his nose made him an easy target for cartoonists.

He was a tireless speaker and the author of innumerable books, including works of theology, literary criticism, history, and travel, as well as novels, short stories, and poetry.

In Father Brown, Chesterton created one of the most unusual and lovable detectives in fiction. The mild-mannered little priest, who at his best combines the perceptiveness of a Sherlock Holmes with an astute knowledge of psychology, has been a favorite with readers for half a century.

THE INVISIBLE MAN

slips past four guards to commit murder!

IN THE COOL blue twilight of two steep streets in Camden Town, the shop at the corner, a confectioner's, glowed like the butt of a cigar. One should rather say, perhaps like the butt of a firework, for the light was of many colors and complexity, broken up by many mirrors and dancing on many gilt and gaily colored cakes and sweetmeats. Against this one fiery glass were glued the noses of many gutter-snipes, for the chocolates were all wrapped in those red and gold and green metallic colors which are almost better than chocolate itself; and the huge white wedding-cake in the window was somehow at once remote and satisfying, just as if the whole North Pole were good to eat. The urchins yearned.

Such rainbow provocations could naturally collect

the youth of the neighborhood up to the ages of ten
or twelve. But this corner was also attractive to youth
at a later stage; and a young man, not less than twenty-
four, was staring into the same shop window. To him,
also, the shop was of fiery charm, but this attraction
was not wholly to be explained by chocolates; which,
however, he was far from despising.

He was a tall, burly, red-haired young man, with a
resolute face but a listless manner. He carried under
his arm a flat, gray portfolio of black-and-white
sketches, which he had sold with more or less success
to publishers ever since his uncle (who was an admiral)
had disinherited him for Socialism, because of a lecture
which he had delivered against that economic theory.
His name was John Turnbull Angus.

Entering at last, he walked through the confectioner's shop into the back room, which was a sort of
pastry-cook restaurant, merely raising his hat to the
young lady who was serving there. She was a dark,
elegant, alert girl in black, with a high color and very
quick, dark eyes; and after the ordinary interval she
followed him into the inner room to take his order.

His order was evidently a usual one. "I want, please,"
he said with precision, "one halfpenny bun and a cup
of black coffee." An instant before the girl could turn
away he added, "Also, I want you to marry me."

The young lady of the shop stiffened suddenly, and
said, "Those are jokes I don't allow."

The red-haired young man lifted gray eyes of an unexpected gravity.

"Really and truly," he said, "it's as serious—as serious as the halfpenny bun. It is expensive, like the bun; one pays for it. It is indigestible, like the bun. It hurts."

The dark young lady had never taken her dark eyes off him, but seemed to be studying him with almost tragic exactitude. At the end of her scrutiny she had something like the shadow of a smile, and she sat down in a chair.

"Don't you think," observed Angus, absently, "that it's rather cruel to eat these halfpenny buns. They might grow up into penny buns. I shall give up these brutal sports when we are married."

The dark young lady rose from her chair and walked to the window, evidently in a state of strong but not unsympathetic cogitation. When at last she swung round again with an air of resolution she was bewildered to observe that the young man was carefully laying out on the table various objects from the shop-window. They included a pyramid of highly colored sweets, several plates of sandwiches, and the two decanters containing that mysterious port and sherry which are peculiar to pastry-cooks. In the middle of this neat arrangement he had carefully let down the enormous load of white sugared cake which had been the huge principal ornament of the window.

"What on earth are you doing?" she asked.

"Duty, my dear Laura," he began.

"Oh, for the Lord's sake, stop a minute," she cried, "and don't talk to me in that way. I mean, what is all that?"

"A ceremonial meal, Miss Hope."

"And what is *that?*" she asked impatiently, pointing to the mountain of sugar.

"The wedding-cake, Mrs. Angus," he said.

The girl marched to that article, removed it with some clatter, and put it back in the shop window; she then returned, and putting her elegant elbows on the table, regarded the young man not unfavorably but with considerable exasperation.

"You don't give me any time to think," she said.

"I'm not such a fool," he answered; "that's my Christian humility."

She was still looking at him; but she had grown considerably graver behind the smile.

"Mr. Angus," she said steadily, "before there is a minute more of this nonsense I must tell you something about myself as shortly as I can."

"Delighted," replied Angus. "You might tell me something about myself, too, while you are about it."

"Oh, do hold your tongue and listen," she said. "It's nothing I'm ashamed of, and it isn't even anything that I'm specially sorry about. But what would you say if there were something that is no business of mine and yet is my nightmare?"

"In that case," said the man seriously, "I should suggest that you bring back the cake."

"Well, you must listen to the story first," said Laura, persistently. "To begin with, I must tell you that my father owned the inn called the 'Red Fish' at Ludbury, and I used to serve people in the bar."

"I have often wondered," he said, "why there was a kind of a Christian air about this one confectioner's shop."

"Ludbury is a sleepy, grassy little hole in the Eastern Counties, and the only kind of people who ever came to the Red Fish were occasional commercial travelers, and for the rest, the most awful people you can see, only you've never seen them. I mean little, loungy men, who had just enough to live on and had nothing to do but lean about in bar-rooms and bet on horses, in bad clothes that were just too good for them. Even these wretched young rotters were not very common at our house; but there were two of them that were a lot too common—common in every sort of way. They both lived on money of their own, and were wearisomely idle and over-dressed. But yet I was a bit sorry for them, because I half believe they slunk into our little empty bar because each of them had a slight deformity; the sort of thing that some yokels laugh at. It wasn't exactly a deformity either; it was more an oddity. One of them was a surprisingly small man, something like a dwarf, or at least like a jockey. He was not at all jockeyish to look at, though; he had a round black head and a well-trimmed black beard, bright eyes like a bird's; he jingled money in his pockets; he jangled a great gold watch chain; and he never turned up except dressed just too much like a gentleman to be one. He was no fool though, though a futile idler; he was curiously clever at all kinds of things that couldn't be the slightest use; a sort of impromptu conjuring; making fifteen matches set fire to each other like a regular firework; or cutting a banana or some such thing into a dancing doll. His name was Isidore Smythe; and I can see him still, with his little dark face just coming up to the counter, making a jumping kangaroo out of five cigars.

"The other fellow was more silent and more ordinary; but somehow he alarmed me much more than poor little Smythe. He was very tall and slight, and light-haired; his nose had a high bridge, and he might almost have been handsome in a spectral sort of way; but he had one of the most appalling squints I have ever seen or heard of. When he looked straight at you, you didn't know where you were yourself, let alone what he was looking at. I fancy this sort of disfigurement embittered the poor chap a little; for while Smythe was ready to show off his monkey tricks anywhere, James Welkin (that was the squinting man's name) never did anything except soak in our bar parlor, and go for great walks by himself in the flat, gray country all 'round. All the same, I think Smythe, too, was a little sensitive about being so small, though he carried it off more smartly. And so it was that I was really puzzled, as well as startled, and very sorry, when they both offered to marry me in the same week.

"Well, I did what I've since thought was perhaps a silly thing. But, after all, these freaks were my friends in a way; and I had a horror of their thinking I refused them for the real reason, which was that they were so impossibly ugly. So I made up some gas of another sort, about never meaning to marry anyone who hadn't carved his way in the world. I said it was a point of principle with me not to live on money that was just inherited like theirs. Two days after I had talked in this well-meaning sort of way, the whole trouble began. The first thing I heard was that both of them had gone off to seek their fortunes, as if they were in some silly fairytale.

"Well, I've never seen either of them from that day to this. But I've had two letters from the little man called Smythe, and really they were rather exciting."

"Ever heard of the other one?" asked Angus.

"No, he never wrote," said the girl, after an instant's hesitation. "Smythe's first letter was simply to say that he started out walking with Welkin to London; but Welkin was such a good walker that the little man dropped out of it, and took a rest by the roadside. He happened to be picked up by some traveling show, and, partly because he was nearly a dwarf, and partly because he was really a clever little wretch, he got on quite well in the show business, and was soon sent up to the Aquarium, to do some tricks that I forget. That was his first letter. His second was much more of a startler, and I only got it last week."

The man called Angus emptied his coffee cup and regarded her with mild and patient eyes. Her own mouth took a slight twist of laughter as she resumed, "I suppose you've seen on the boardings all about this 'Smythe's Silent Service'? Or you must be the only person that hasn't. Oh, I don't know much about it, it's some clockwork invention for doing all the housework by machinery. You know the sort of thing; "Press a button—A Butler who Never Drinks.' 'Turn a Handle —Ten Housemaids who Never Flirt.' You must have seen the advertisements. Well, whatever these machines are, they are making pots of money; and they are making it all for this little imp whom I knew down in Ludbury. I can't help feeling pleased the poor little chap has fallen on his feet; but the plain fact is, I'm in terror of his turning up any minute and telling me he's carved his way in the world—as he certainly has."

"And the other man?" repeated Angus with a sort of obstinate quietude.

Laura Hope got to her feet suddenly. "My friend," she said, "I think you are a witch. Yes, you are quite right. I have not seen a line of the other man's writing; and I have no more notion than the dead of what or where he is. But it is of him that I am frightened. It is he who is all about my path. It is he who has half driven me mad. Indeed, I think he has driven me mad; for I have felt him where he could not have been, and I have heard his voice when he could not have spoken."

"Well, my dear," said the young man, cheerfully, "if he were Satan himself, he is done for now you have told somebody. One goes mad all alone, old girl. But when was it you fancied you felt and heard our squinting friend?"

"I heard James Welkin laugh as plainly as I hear you speak," said the girl, steadily. "There was nobody there, for I stood just outside the shop at the corner, and could see down both streets at once. I had forgotten how he laughed, though his laugh was as odd as his squint. I had not thought of him for nearly a year. But it's a solemn truth that a few seconds later the first letter came from his rival."

"Did you ever make the spectre speak or squeak, or anything?" asked Angus, with some interest.

Laura suddenly shuddered, and then said, with an unshaken voice, "Yes. Just when I had finished reading the second letter from Isidore Smythe announcing his success, just then, I heard Welkin say, 'He shan't have you, though.' It was quite plain, as if he were in the room. It is awful; I think I must be mad."

"If you really were mad," said the young man, "you would think you must be sane. But certainly there seems to me to be something a little rum about this unseen gentleman. Two heads are better than one—I spare you allusions to any other organs—and really, if you would allow me, as a sturdy, practical man, to bring back the wedding-cake out of the window ——"

Even as he spoke, there was a sort of steely shriek in the street outside, and a small motor, driven at devilish speed, shot up to the door of the shop and stuck there. In the same flash of time a small man in a shiny top hat stood stamping in the outer room.

Angus, who had hitherto maintained hilarious ease from motives of mental hygiene, revealed the strain of his soul by striding abruptly out of the inner room and confronting the new-comer. A glance at him was quite sufficient to confirm the savage guesswork of a man in

love. This very dapper but dwarfish figure, with the
spike of black beard carried insolently forward, the
clever unrestful eyes, the neat but very nervous fingers,
could be none other than the man just described to him:
Isidore Smythe, who made dolls out of banana skins
and match-boxes; Isidore Smythe, who made millions
out of undrinking butlers and unflirting housemaids of
metal. For a moment the two men, instinctively understanding each other's air of possession, looked at each
other with that curious cold generosity which is the
soul of rivalry.

Mr. Smythe, however, made no allusion to the ulti-
mate ground of their antagonism, but said simply and
explosively, "Has Miss Hope seen that thing on the
window?"

"On the window?" repeated the staring Angus.

"There's no time to explain other things," said the
small millionaire shortly. "There's some   tomfoolery
going on here that has to be investigated."

He pointed his polished walking-stick at the window, recently depleted by the bridal preparations of
Mr. Angus; and that gentleman was astonished to see
along the front of the glass a long strip of paper pasted,
which had certainly not been on the window when he
looked through it some time before. Following the
energetic Smythe outside into the street, he found that
some yard and a half of stamp-paper had been carefully
gummed along the glass outside, and on this was written in straggly characters, "If you marry Smythe, he
will die."

"Laura," said Angus, putting his big red head into the shop, "you're not mad."

"It's the writing of that fellow Welkin," said Smythe, gruffly. "I haven't seen him for years, but he's always bothering me. Five times in the last fortnight he's had threatening letters left at my flat, and I can't even find out who leaves them, let alone if it is Welkin himself. The porter of the flat swears that no suspicious characters have been seen, and here he has pasted up a sort of dado on a public shop window, while the people in the shop ——"

"Quite so," said Angus, modestly, "while the people in the shop were having tea. Well, sir, I can assure you I appreciate your common sense in dealing so directly with the matter. We can talk about other things afterwards. The fellow cannot be very far off yet, for I swear there was no paper there when I went last to the window, ten or fifteen minutes ago. On the other hand, he's too far off to be chased, as we don't even know the direction. If you'll take my advice, Mr. Smythe, you'll put this at once in the hands of some energetic inquiry man, private rather than public. I know an extremely clever fellow, who has set up in business five minutes from here in your car. His name's Flambeau, and though his youth was a bit stormy, he's a strictly honest man now, and his brains are worth money. He lives in Lucknow Mansions, Hampstead."

"That is odd," said the little man, arching his black eyebrows. "I live, myself, in Himalaya Mansions, 'round the corner. Perhaps you might care to come with me; I can go to my rooms and sort out these queer Welkin documents, while you run 'round and get your friend the detective."

"You are very good," said Angus, politely. "Well, the sooner we act the better."

Both men, with a queer kind of impromptu fairness, took the same sort of formal farewell of the lady, and both jumped into the brisk little car. As Smythe took the handles and they turned the great corner of the street, Angus was amused to see a gigantesque poster of "Smythe's Silent Service," with a picture of a huge headless iron doll, carrying a saucepan with the legend, "A Cook Who is Never Cross."

"I use them in my own flat," said the little black-bearded man, laughing, "partly for advertisement, and partly for real convenience. Honestly, and all above board, those big clockwork dolls of mine do bring you coals or claret or a time table quicker than any live servants I've ever known, if you know which knob to press. But I'll never deny, between ourselves that such servants have their disadvantages, too."

"Indeed?" said Angus; "is there something they can't do?"

"Yes," replied Smythe, coolly; "they can't tell me who left those threatening letters at my flat."

The man's motor was small and swift like himself; in fact, like his domestic service, it was of his own invention. If he was an advertising quack, he was one who believed in his own wares. The sense of something tiny and flying was accentuated as they swept up long

white curves of road in the dead but open daylight of
evening. Soon the white curves came sharper and diz-
zier; they were upon ascending spirals, as they say in
the modern religions. For, indeed, they were cresting
a corner of London which is almost as precipitous as
Edinburgh, if not quite so picturesque. Terrace rose
above terrace, and the special tower of flats they sought
rose above them all to almost Egyptian height, gilt by
the level sunset. The change, as they turned the corner
and entered the crescent known as Himalaya Mansions,
was as abrupt as the opening of a window; for they
found that pile of flats sitting above London as above
a green sea of slate. Opposite to the mansions, on the
other side of the gravel crescent, was a bushy enclosure
more like a steep hedge or dyke than a garden, and
some way below that ran a strip of artificial water, a
sort of canal, like the moat of that embowered fortress.
As the car swept 'round the crescent it passed, at one
corner, the stray stall of a man selling chestnuts; and
right away at the other end of the curve, Angus could
see a dim blue policeman walking slowly. These were
the only human shapes in that high suburban solitude;
but he had an irrational sense that they expressed the
speechless poetry of London. He felt as if they were
figures in a story.

The little car shot up to the right house like a bullet,
and shot out its owner like a bomb shell. He was immediately inquiring of a tall commissionaire in shining
braid, and a short porter in shirt sleeves, whether anybody or anything had been seeking his apartments. He

was assured that nobody and nothing had passed these officials since his last inquiries; whereupon he and the slightly bewildered Angus were shot up in the lift like a rocket, till they reached the top floor.

"Just come in for a minute," said the breathless Smythe. "I want to show you those Welkin letters. Then you might run 'round the corner and fetch your friend." He pressed a button concealed in the wall, and the door opened of itself.

It opened on a long, commodious ante-room, of which the only arresting features, ordinarily speaking, were the rows of tall half-human mechanical figures that stood up on both sides like tailors' dummies. Like tailors' dummies they were headless; and like tailors' dummies they had a handsome unnecessary bumpiness in the shoulders, and a pigeon-breasted protuberance of chest; but barring this, they were not much more like a human figure than any automatic machine at a station that is about the human height. They had two great hooks like arms, for carrying trays; and they were painted pea-green, or vermilion, or black for convenience of distinction; in every other way they were only automatic machines and nobody would have looked twice at them. On this occasion, at least, nobody did. For between the two rows of these domestic dummies lay something more interesting than most of the mechanics of the world. It was a white, tattered scrap of paper scrawled with red ink; and the agile inventor had snatched it up almost as soon as the door flew open. He handed it to Angus without a word. The red ink on it actually was not dry, and the message ran, "If you have seen her today, I shall kill you."

There was a short silence, and then Isidore Smythe said quietly, "Would you like a little whisky? I rather feel as if I should."

"Thank you; I should like a little Flambeau," said Angus, gloomily. "This business seems to me to be getting rather grave. I'm going 'round at once to fetch him."

"Right you are," said the other, with admirable cheerfulness. "Bring him here as quick as you can."

But as Angus closed the front door behind him he saw Smythe push back a button, and one of the clock-work images glided from its place and slid along a groove in the floor carrying a tray with siphon and decanter. There did seem something a trifle weird about leaving the little man alone among those dead servants, who were coming to life as the door closed.

Six steps down from Smythe's landing the man in shirt sleeves was doing something with a pail. Angus stopped to extract a promise, fortified with a prospective bribe, that he would remain in that place until the return with the detective, and would keep count of any kind of stranger coming up those stairs. Dashing down to the front hall he then laid similar charges of vigilance on the commissionaire at the front door, from whom he learned the simplifying circumstances that there was no back door. Not content with this, he captured the floating policeman and induced him to stand opposite the entrance and watch it; and finally

paused an instant for a penny-worth of chestnuts, and
an inquiry as to the probable length of the merchant's
stay in the neighborhood.

The chestnut seller, turning up the collar of his coat,
told him he should probably be moving shortly, as he
thought it was going to snow. Indeed, the evening was
growing gray and bitter, but Angus, with all his elo-
quence, proceeded to nail the chestnut man to his post.

"Keep yourself warm on your own chestnuts," he
said earnestly. "Eat up your whole stock; I'll make it
worth your while. I'll give you a sovereign if you'll
wait here till I come back, and then tell me whether
any man, woman, or child has gone into that house
where the commissionaire is standing."

He then walked away smartly, with a last look at
the besieged tower.

"I've made a ring 'round that room, anyhow," he
said. "They can't all four of them be Mr. Welkin's
accomplices."

Lucknow Mansions were, so to speak, on a lower
platform of that hill of houses, of which Himalaya
Mansions might be called the peak. Mr. Flambeau's
semi-official flat was on the ground floor, and presented
in every way a marked contrast to the American machinery and cold hotel-like luxury of the flat of the
Silent Service. Flambeau, who was a friend of Angus,
received him in a rococo artistic den behind his office,
of which the ornaments were sabres, harquebuses, Eastern curiosities, flasks of Italian wine, savage cooking
pots, a plumy Persian cat, and a small dusty-looking

Roman Catholic priest, who looked particularly out of place.

"This is my friend Father Brown," said Flambeau. "I've often wanted you to meet him. Splendid weather, this; a little cold for Southerners like me."

"Yes, I think it will keep clear," said Angus, sitting down on a violet-striped Eastern ottoman.

"No," said the priest quietly, "it has begun to snow."

And indeed, as he spoke, the first few flakes, foreseen by the man of chestnuts, began to drift across the darkening window-pane.

"Well," said Angus, heavily, "I'm afraid I've come on business, and rather jumpy business at that. The fact is, Flambeau, within a stone's throw of your house is a fellow who badly wants your help; he's perpetually being haunted and threatened by an invisible enemy— a scoundrel whom nobody has ever seen." As Angus proceeded to tell the whole tale of Smythe and Welkin, beginning with Laura's story, and going on with his own, the supernatural laugh at the corner of two empty streets, the strange distinct words spoken in an empty room, Flambeau grew more and more vividly concerned, and the little priest seemed to be left out of it, like a piece of furniture. When it came to the scribbled stamp-paper pasted on the window, Flambeau rose, seeming to fill the room with his huge shoulders.

"If you don't mind," he said, "I think you had better tell me the rest on the nearest road to this man's house. It strikes me, somehow, that there is no time to be lost."

"Delighted," said Angus, rising also, "though he's safe enough for the present, for I've set four men to watch the only hole to his burrow."

They turned out into the street, the small priest trundling after them with the docility of a small dog. He merely said, in a cheerful way, like one making conversation, "How quick the snow gets thick on the ground."

As they threaded the steep side streets already powdered with silver, Angus finished his story; and by the time they reached the crescent with the towering flats, he had leisure to turn his attention to the four sentinels. The chestnut seller, both before and after receiving a sovereign, swore stubbornly that he had watched the door and seen no visitor enter. The policeman was even more emphatic. He said he had had experience of crooks of all kinds, in top hats and in rags; he wasn't so green as to suspect suspicious characters to look suspicious; he looked out for anybody, and, so help him, there had been nobody. And when all three men gathered 'round the gilded commissionaire, who still stood smiling astride of the porch, the verdict was more final still.

"I've got a right to ask any man, duke or dustman, what he wants in these flats," said the genial and gold-laced giant, "and I'll swear there's been nobody to ask since this gentleman went away."

The unimportant Father Brown, who stood back, looking modestly at the pavement, here ventured to say meekly, "Has nobody been up and down stairs, then, since the snow began to fall? It began while we were all 'round at Flambeau's.''

"Nobody's been in here, sir, you can take it from me," said the official, with beaming authority.

"Then I wonder what that is?" said the priest, and stared at the ground blankly like a fish.

The others all looked down also; and Flambeau used a fierce exclamation and a French gesture. For it was unquestionably true that down the middle of the entrance guarded by the man in gold lace, actually between the arrogant, stretched legs of that colossus, ran a stringy pattern of gray footprints stamped upon the white snow.

"God!" cried Angus, involuntarily, "the Invisible Man!"

Without another word he turned and dashed up the stairs, with Flambeau following; but Father Brown still stood looking about him in the snow-clad street as if he had lost interest in his query.

Flambeau was plainly in a mood to break down the door with his big shoulder; but the Scotsman, with more reason, if less intuition, fumbled about on the frame of the door till he found the invisible button; and the door swung slowly open.

It showed substantially the same serried interior; the hall had grown darker, though it was still struck here and there with the last crimson shafts of sunset, and one or two of the headless machines had been moved from their places for this or that purpose, and stood here and there about the twilit place. The green and red of their coats were all darkened in the dusk; and their likeness to human shapes slightly increased by their very shapelessness. But in the middle of them all, exactly where the paper with the red ink had lain, there lay something that looked very like red ink spilt out of its bottle. But it was not red ink.

With a French combination of reason and violence Flambeau simply said "Murder!" and, plunging into the flat, had explored every corner and cupboard of it in five minutes. But if he expected to find a corpse he found none. Isidore Smythe simply was not in the place, either dead or alive. After the most tearing search the two men met each other in the outer hall, with streaming faces and staring eyes. "My friend," said Flambeau, talking French in his excitement, "not only is your murderer invisible, but he makes invisible also the murdered man."

Angus looked 'round at the dim room full of dummies, and in some Celtic corner of his Scotch soul a shudder started. One of the life-size dolls stood immediately overshadowing the blood stain, summoned, perhaps, by the slain man an instant before he fell. One of the high-shouldered hooks that served the thing for arms was a little lifted, and Angus had suddenly the horrid fancy that poor Smythe's own iron child had struck him down. Matter had rebelled, and these machines had killed their master. But even so, what had they done with him?

"Eaten him?" said the nightmare in his ear; and he sickened for an instant at the idea of rent, human remains absorbed and crushed into all that acephalous clockwork.

He recovered his mental health by an emphatic effort, and said to Flambeau, "Well, there it is. The poor fellow has evaporated like a cloud and left a red streak on the floor. The tale does not belong to this world."

"There is only one thing to be done," said Flambeau, "whether it belongs to this world or the other, I must go down and talk to my friend."

They descended, passing the man with the pail, who again asseverated that he had let no intruder pass, down to the commissionaire and the hovering chestnut man, who rigidly reasserted their own watchfulness. But when Angus looked 'round for his fourth confirmation he could not see it, and called out with some nervousness, "Where is the policeman?"

"I beg your pardon," said Father Brown; "that is my fault. I just sent him down the road to investigate something—that I thought worth investigating."

"Well, we want him back pretty soon," said Angus, abruptly, "for the wretched man upstairs has not only been murdered but wiped out."

"How?" asked the priest.

"Father," said Flambeau, after a pause, "upon my soul I believe it is more in your department than mine. No friend or foe has entered the house, but Smythe is gone, as if stolen by the fairies. If that is not supernatural, I ——"

As he spoke they were all checked by an unusual sight; the big blue policeman came 'round the corner of the crescent, running. He came straight up to Brown.

"You're right, sir," he panted, "they've just found poor Mr. Smythe's body in the canal down below."

Angus put his hand wildly to his head. "Did he run down and drown himself?" he asked.

"He never came down, I'll swear," said the constable, "and he wasn't drowned either, for he died of a great stab over the heart."

"And yet you saw no one enter?" said Flambeau in a grave voice.

"Let us walk down the road a little," said the priest.

As they reached the other end of the crescent he observed abruptly, "Stupid of me! I forgot to ask the policeman something. I wonder if they found a light brown sack."

"Why a light brown sack?" asked Angus.

"Because if it was any other colored sack, the case must begin over again," said Father Brown; "but if it was a light brown sack, why, the case is finished."

"I am pleased to hear it," said Angus with hearty irony. "It hasn't begun, so far as I am concerned."

"You must tell us all about it," said Flambeau with a strange heavy simplicity, like a child.

Unconsciously they were walking with quickening steps down the long sweep of road on the other side of the high crescent, Father Brown leading briskly, though in silence. At last he said with an almost touching vagueness, "Well, I'm afraid you'll think it so prosy. We always begin at the abstract end of things, and you can't begin this story anywhere else.

"Have you ever noticed this—that people never answer what you say? They answer what you mean—or what they think you mean. Suppose one lady says to another in a country house, 'Is anybody staying with you?' the lady doesn't answer 'Yes; the butler, the three footmen, the parlormaid, and so on,' though the parlormaid may be in the room, or the butler behind her chair. She says 'There is *nobody* staying with us,' meaning nobody of the sort you mean. But suppose a doctor inquiring into an epidemic asks, 'Who is staying in the house?' then the lady will remember the butler, the parlormaid, and the rest. All language is used like that; you never get a question answered literally, even when you get it answered truly. When those four quite honest men said that no man had gone into the Mansions, they did not really mean that *no man* had gone into them. They meant no man whom they could suspect of being your man. A man did go into the house, and did come out of it, but they never noticed him."

"An invisible man?" inquired Angus, raising his red eyebrows.

"A mentally invisible man," said Father Brown.

A minute or two after he resumed in the same unassuming voice, like a man thinking his way. "Of course, you can't think of such a man, until you do think of him. That's where his cleverness comes in. But I came to think of him through two or three things in the tale Mr. Angus told us. First, there was the fact that this Welkin went for long walks. And then was the vast lot of stamp-paper on the window. And

then, most of all, there were the two things the young
lady said—things that couldn't be true. Don't get annoyed," he added hastily, noting a sudden movement
of the Scotsman's head; "she thought they were true
all right, but they couldn't be true. A person *can't* be
quite alone in a street a second before she receives a
letter. She can't be quite alone in a street when she
starts reading a letter just received. There must be
somebody pretty near her; he must be mentally invisible."

"Why must there be somebody near her?" asked
Angus.

"Because," said Father Brown, "barring carrier-
pigeons, somebody must have brought her the letter."

"Do you really mean to say," asked Flambeau, "that
Welkin carried his rival's letters to his lady?"

"Yes," said the priest. "Welkin carried his rival's
letters to his lady. You see, he had to."

"Oh, I can't stand much more of this," exploded
Flambeau. "Who is this fellow? What does he look
like? What is the usual get-up of a mentally invisible
man?"

"He is dressed rather handsomely in red, blue and
gold," replied the priest promptly with precision, "and
in this striking, and even showy, costume he entered
Himalaya Mansions under eight human eyes; he killed
Smythe in cold blood, and came down into the street
again carrying the dead body in his arms ——"

"Reverend sir," cried Angus, standing still, "are you
raving mad, or am I?"

"You are not mad," said Brown, "only a little un-observant. You have not noticed such a man as this, for example."

He took three quick strides forward, and put his hand on the shoulder of an ordinary passing postman who had bustled by them unnoticed under the shade of the trees.

"Nobody ever notices postmen somehow," he said thoughtfully; "yet they have passions like other men, and even carry large bags where a small corpse can be stowed quite easily."

The postman, instead of turning naturally, had ducked and tumbled against the garden fence. He was a lean fair-bearded man of very ordinary appearance but as he turned an alarmed face over his shoulder, all three men were fixed with an almost fiendish squint.

Flambeau went back to his sabres, purple rugs and Persian cat, having many things to attend to. John Turnbull Angus went back to the lady at the shop, with whom that imprudent young man contrives to be extremely comfortable. But Father Brown walked those snow-covered hills under the stars for many hours with a murderer, and what they said to each other will never be known.

JOHN D. MACDONALD

. . . was born in Pennsylvania in 1916. He took his Masters degree at the Harvard School of Business Administration. During World War II, MacDonald joined the Army and rose to the rank of colonel. While serving in the Army, he wrote a story and sent it to his wife asking her to try and sell it. She did.

After the war, he decided to try writing for a year to see if he could make a living out of it. Since then, he has written 40 novels and over 500 short stories.

"The Homesick Buick," one of MacDonald's best tales, is a fast-paced account of a daring bank robbery which had the police and a whole town completely baffled. No one can learn anything from the getaway car, the sole stolid uncommunicative clue. A young teen-ager calmly shows them the way and we have an enthralling yarn.

A daring bank robbery baffles the police
but a teen-age boy diagnoses

THE HOMESICK BUICK

and traces the criminals' hide-out

TO GET TO LEEMAN, TEXAS, you go southwest from Beaumont on Route 90 for approximately thirty miles and then turn right on a two-lane concrete farm road. Five minutes from the time you turn, you will reach Leeman. The main part of town is six lanes wide and five blocks long. If the hand of a careless giant should remove the six gas stations, the two theaters, Willows' Hardware Store, the Leeman National Bank, the two big air-conditioned five-and-dimes, the Sears' store, four cafés, Rightsinger's dress shop, and The Leeman House, a twenty-room hotel, there would be very little left except the supermarket and four drugstores.

On October 3, 1949, a Mr. Stanley Woods arrived by bus and carried his suitcase over to The Leeman

House. In Leeman there is no social distinction of bus,
train, or plane, since Leeman has neither airport facili-
ties nor railroad station.

On all those who were questioned later, Mr. Stanley
Woods seemed to have made very little impression.
They all spoke of kind of a medium-sized fella in his
thirties, or it might be his forties. No, he wasn't fat,
but he wasn't thin either. Blue eyes? Could be brown.
Wore a gray suit, I think. Can't remember whether his
glasses had rims or not. If they did have, they were
probably gold.

But all were agreed that Mr. Stanley Woods radiated
quiet confidence and the smell of money. According
to the cards that were collected here and there, Mr.
Woods represented the Groston Precision Tool Company of Atlanta, Georgia. He had deposited in the
Leeman National a certified check for twelve hundred
dollars, and the bank had made the routine check of
looking up the credit standing of Groston. It was Dun
& Bradstreet double-A, but, of course, the company explained later that they had never heard of Mr. Stanley
Woods. Nor could the fake calling cards be traced.
They were of a type of paper and type face which
could be duplicated sixty or a hundred times in every
big city in the country.

Mr. Woods' story, which all agreed on, was that he
was " . . . nosing around to find a good location for a
small plant. Decentralization, you know. No, we don't
want it right in town."

He rented Tod Bishner's car during the day. Tod

works at the Shell station on the corner of Beaumont and Lone Star Streets and doesn't have any use for his Plymouth sedan during the day. Mr. Woods drove around all the roads leading out of town, and, of course, real estate prices were jacked to a considerable degree during his stay.

Mr. Stanley Woods left Leeman rather suddenly on the morning of October 17, under unusual circumstances.

The first person to note a certain oddness was Miss Trilla Price on the switchboard at the phone company. Her local calls were all right, but she couldn't place Charley Anderson's call to Houston, nor, when she tried, could she raise Beaumont. Charley was upset because he wanted to wangle an invitation to go visit his sister over the coming week end.

That was at five minutes of nine. It was probably at the same time that a car with two men in it parked on Beaumont Street, diagonally across from the bank, and one of the two men lifted the hood and began to fiddle with the electrical system.

Nobody agrees from what direction the Buick came into town. There were a man and a girl in it, and they parked near the drugstore. No one seems to know where the third car parked, or even what kind of car it was.

The girl and the man got out of the Buick slowly, just as Stanley Woods came down the street from the hotel.

In Leeman the bank is open on weekdays from nine

until two. And so, at nine o'clock, C. F. Hethridge, who is, or was, the chief teller, raised the green shades on the inside of the bank doors and unlocked the doors. He greeted Mr. Woods, who went on over to the high counter at the east wall and began to ponder over his checkbook.

At this point, out on the street, a very peculiar thing happened. One of the two men in the first car strolled casually over and stood beside the Buick. The other man started the motor of the first car, drove down the street, and made a wide U-turn to swing in and park behind the Buick.

The girl and the man had gone over to Bob Kimball's window. Bob is second teller, and the only thing he can remember about the girl is that she was blonde and a little hard-looking around the mouth, and that she wore a great big alligator shoulder bag. The man with her made no impression on Bob at all, except that Bob thinks the man was on the heavy side.

Old Rod Harrigan, the bank guard, was standing beside the front door, yawning, and picking his teeth with a broken match.

At this point, C. F. Hethridge heard the buzzer on the big time vault and went over and swung the door wide and went in to get the money for the cages. He was out almost immediately, carrying Bob's tray over to him. The girl was saying something about cashing a check, and Bob had asked her for identification. She had opened the big shoulder bag as her escort strolled over to the guard. At the same moment the girl pulled out a small, vicious-looking revolver and aimed it between Bob's eyes, her escort sapped old Rod Harrigan with such gusto that it was four that same afternoon before he came out of it enough to talk. And then, of course, he knew nothing.

C. F. Hethridge bolted for the vault, and Bob, wondering whether he should step on the alarm, looked over the girl's shoulder just in time to see Stanley Woods aim carefully and bring Hethridge down with a slug through the head, catching him on the fly, so to speak.

Bob says that things were pretty confusing and that the sight of Hethridge dying so suddenly sort of took the heart out of him. Anyway, there was a third car and it contained three men, two of them equipped with empty black-leather suitcases. They went into the vault, acting as though they had been all through the bank fifty times. They stepped over Hethridge on the way in, and on the way out again.

About the only cash they overlooked was the cash right in front of Bob, in his teller's drawer.

As they all broke for the door, Bob dropped and pressed the alarm button. He said later that he held his hands over his eyes, though what good that would do him, he couldn't say.

Henry Willows is the real hero. He was fuddying around in his hardware store when he heard the alarm. With a reaction time remarkable in a man close to seventy, he took a little .22 rifle, slapped a clip into it, trotted to his store door, and quickly analyzed the situation. He saw Mr. Woods, whom he recognized, plus three strangers and a blonde woman coming out of the bank pretty fast. Three cars were lined up, each one with a driver. Two of the men coming out of the bank carried heavy suitcases. Henry leveled on the driver of the lead car, the Buick, and shot him in the left temple, killing him outright. The man slumped over the wheel, his body resting against the horn ring, which, of course, added its blare to the clanging of the bank alarm.

At that point a slug, later identified as having come from a Smith & Wesson Police Positive, smashed a neat hole in Henry's plate-glass store window, radiating cracks in all directions. Henry ducked, and by the time he got ready to take a second shot, the two other cars were gone. The Buick was still there. He saw Bob run out of the bank, and later on he told his wife that he had his finger on the trigger and his sights lined up before it came to him that it was Bob Kimball.

It was agreed that the two cars headed out toward Route 90, and within two minutes Hod Abrams and Lefty Quinn had roared out of town in the same direction in the only police car. They were followed by belligerent amateurs to whom Henry Willows had doled out firearms. But on the edge of town all cars ran into an odd obstacle. The road was liberally sprinkled with metal objects shaped exactly like the jacks that little girls pick up when they bounce a ball, except they were four times normal size and all the points were sharpened. No matter how a tire hit one, it was certain to be punctured.

The police car swerved to a screaming stop, nearly tipping over. The Stein twins, boys of nineteen, managed to avoid the jacks in their souped-up heap until they were hitting eighty. When they finally hit one, the heap rolled over an estimated ten times, killing the twins outright.

So that made four dead. Hethridge, the Stein twins, and one unidentified bank robber.

Nobody wanted to touch the robber, and he stayed right where he was until the battery almost ran down and the horn squawked into silence. Hod Abrams commandeered a car, and he and Lefty rode back into town and took charge. They couldn't get word out by phone, and within a very short time they found that some sharpshooter with a high-powered rifle had gone to work on the towers of local station WLEE and had put the station out of business.

Thus, by the time the Texas Rangers were alerted and ready to set up road blocks, indecision and confusion had permitted an entire hour to pass.

The Houston office of the FBI assigned a detail of men to the case, and from the Washington headquarters, two bank-robbery experts were dispatched by plane to Beaumont. Reporters came from Houston and Beaumont and the two national press services, and Leeman found itself on the front pages all over the country because the planning behind the job seemed to fascinate the average joe.

Mr. Woods left town on that particular Thursday

morning. The FBI from Houston was there by noon, and the Washington contingent arrived late Friday. Everyone was very confident. There were a corpse and a car to work on. These would certainly provide the necessary clues to indicate which outfit had pulled the job, even though the method of the robbery did not point to any particular group whose habits were known.

Investigation headquarters were set up in the local police station, and Hod and Lefty, very important in the beginning, had to stand around outside trying to look as though they knew what was going on.

Hethridge, who had been a cold, reserved, unpopular man, had, within twenty-four hours, fifty stories invented about his human kindness and generosity. The Stein twins, heretofore considered to be trash who would be better off in prison, suddenly became proper sons of old Texas.

Special Agent Randolph A. Sternweister, who, fifteen years before, had found a law office to be a dull place, was in charge of the case, being the senior of the two experts who had flown down from Washington. He was forty-one years old, a chain smoker, a chubby man with incongruous hollow cheeks and hair of a shade of gray which his wife, Claire, tells him is distinguished.

The corpse was the first clue. Age, between thirty and thirty-two. Brown hair, thinning on top. Good teeth, with only four small cavities, two of them filled. Height, five feet eight and a quarter; weight, a hundred and forty-eight. No distinguishing scars or tattoos. X-ray plates showed that the right arm had been fractured years before. His clothes were neither new nor old. The suit had been purchased in Chicago. The shirt, underwear, socks, and shoes were all national brands, in the medium-price range. In his pockets they found an almost full pack of cigarettes, a battered Zippo lighter, three fives and a one in a cheap trick billclip, eighty-five cents in change, a book of matches advertising a nationally known laxative, a white bone button, two wooden kitchen matches with blue-and-white heads, and a penciled map, on cheap notebook paper, of the main drag of Leeman—with no indication as to escape route. His fingerprint classification was teletyped to the Central Bureau files, and the answer came back that there was no record of him. It was at this point that fellow workers noted that Mr. Sternweister became a shade irritable.

The next search of the corpse was more minute. No specific occupational calluses were found on his hands. The absence of laundry marks indicated that his linen, if it had been sent out, had been cleaned by a neighborhood laundress. Since Willows had used a .22 hollow-point, the hydraulic pressure on the brain fluids had caused the eyes of Mr. X to bulge in a disconcerting fashion. A local undertaker, experienced in the damage caused by the average Texas automobile accident, replaced the bulging eyeballs and smoothed out the expression for a series of pictures which were sent to many points. The Chicago office reported that the

clothing store which had sold the suit was large and
that the daily traffic was such that no clerk could identify the customer from the picture; nor was the young-
ish man known to the Chicago police.

Fingernail scrapings were put in a labeled glassine
envelope, as well as the dust vacuumed from pants'
cuffs and other portions of the clothing likely to collect
dust. The excellent lab in Houston reported back that
the dust and scrapings were negative to the extent that
the man could not be tied down to any particular locality.

In the meantime the Buick had been the object of
equal scrutiny. The outside was a mass of prints from
the citizens of Leeman who had peered morbidly in at
the man leaning against the horn ring. The plates were
Mississippi license plates, and in checking with the
Bureau of Motor Vehicle Registration, it was found
that the plates had been issued for a 1949 Mercury
convertible which had been almost totally destroyed in
a head-on collision in June, 1949. The motor number
and serial number of the Buick were checked against
central records, and it was discovered that the Buick
was one which had disappeared from Chapel Hill,
North Carolina, on the 5th of July, 1949. The insur-
ance company, having already replaced the vehicle, was
anxious to take possession of the stolen car.

Pictures of Mr. X, relayed to Chapel Hill, North
Carolina, and to myriad points in Mississippi, drew a
large blank. In the meantime a careful dusting of the
car had brought out six prints, all different. Two of

them turned out to be on record. The first was on record through the cross-classification of Army prints. The man in question was found working in a gas station in Lake Charles, Louisiana. He had a very difficult two hours until a bright police officer had him demonstrate his procedure for brushing out the front of a car. Ex-Sergeant Golden braced his left hand against the dashboard in almost the precise place where the print had been found. He was given a picture of Mr. X to study. By that time he was so thoroughly annoyed at the forces of law and order that it was impossible to ascertain whether or not he had ever seen the man in question. But due to the apparent freshness of the paint, it was established—a reasonable assumption—that the gangsters had driven into Texas from the East.

The second print on record was an old print, visible when dust was carefully blown off the braces under the dismantled front seat. It belonged to a garage mechanic in Chapel Hill, who once had a small misunderstanding with the forces of law and order and who was able to prove, through the garage work orders, that he had repaired the front-seat mechanism when it had jammed in April, 1949.

The samples of road dirt and dust taken from the fender wells and the frame members proved nothing. The dust was proved, spectroscopically, to be from deep in the heart of Texas, and the valid assumption, after checking old weather reports, was that the car had come through some brisk thunderstorms en route.

Butts in the ash try of the car showed that either two

women, or one woman with two brands of lipstick, had ridden recently as a passenger. Both brands of lipstick were of shades which would go with a fair-complexioned blonde, and both brands were available in Woolworth's, Kress', Kresge's, Walgreen's—in fact, in every chain outfit of any importance.

One large crumb of stale whole-wheat bread was found on the floor mat, and even Sternweister could make little of that, despite the fact that the lab was able to report that the bread had been eaten in conjunction with liverwurst.

Attention was given to the oversized jacks which had so neatly punctured the tires. An ex-OSS officer reported that similar items had been scattered on enemy roads in Burma during the late war, and after examining the samples, he stated confidently that the OSS merchandise had been better made. A competent machinist looked them over and stated with assurance that they had been made by cutting eighth-inch rods into short lengths, grinding them on a wheel, putting them in a jig, and spot-welding them. He said that the maker did not do much of a job on either the grinding or the welding, and that the jig itself was a little out of line. An analysis of the steel showed that it was a Jones & Laughlin product that could be bought in quantity at any wholesaler and in a great many hardware stores.

The auditors, after a careful examination of the situation at the bank, reported that the sum of exactly $94,725 had disappeared. They recommended that the balance of $982.80 remaining in Stanley Woods' account be considered as forfeited, thus reducing the loss to $93,742.20. The good citizens of Leeman preferred to think that Stanley had withdrawn his account.

Every person who had a glimpse of the gang was cross-examined. Sternweister was appalled at the difficulty involved in even establishing how many there had been. Woods, the blonde, and the stocky citizen were definite. And then there were two with suitcases —generally agreed upon. Total, so far—five. The big question was whether each car had a driver waiting. Some said no—that the last car in line had been empty. Willows insisted angrily that there had been a driver behind each wheel. Sternweister at last settled for a total of eight, seven of whom escaped.

No one had taken down a single license number. But it was positively established that the other two cars had been either two- or four-door sedans in dark blue, black, green, or maroon, and that they had been either Buicks, Nashes, Oldsmobiles, Chryslers, Pontiacs or Packards—or maybe Hudsons. And one lone woman held out for convertible Cadillacs. For each person that insisted that they had Mississippi registration, there was one equally insistent on Louisiana, Texas, Alabama, New Mexico, and Oklahoma. And one old lady said that she guessed she knew a California plate when she saw one.

On Saturday morning, nine days after the sudden blow to the FDIC, Randolph Sternweister paced back and forth in his suite at the hotel, which he shared with the number-two man from the Washington end, one Buckley Weed. Weed was reading through the transcripts of the testimony of the witnesses, in vain hope of finding something to which insufficient importance had been given. Weed, though lean, a bit stooped, and only thirty-one, had, through osmosis, acquired most of the personal mannerisms of his superior. Sternweister had noticed this and for the past year had been on the verge of mentioning it. As Weed had acquired Sternweister's habit of lighting one cigarette off the last half-inch of the preceding one, any room in which the two of them remained for more than an hour took on the look and smell of any hotel room after a Legion convention.

"Nothing," Sternweister said. "Not one censored, unmentionable, unprintable, unspeakable thing! My God, if I ever want to kill anybody, I'll do it in the Pennsy Station at five-fifteen."

"Yes, at five-fifteen," said Weed.

"The Bureau has cracked cases when the only thing it had to go on was a human hair or a milligram of dust. My God, we've got a whole automobile that weighs nearly two tons, and a whole corpse! They'll think we're down here learning to rope calves. You know what?"

"What, Ran?"

"I think this was done by a bunch of amateurs. There ought to be a law restricting the practice of crime to professionals. A bunch of wise amateurs. And you can bet your loudest argyles, my boy, that they established identity, hide-out, the works, before they knocked off that vault. Right now, blast their souls, they're being seven average citizens in some average community, making no splash with that ninety-four grand. People didn't used to move around so much. Since the war they've been migrating all over the place. See anything in those transcripts?"

"Nothing."

"Then stop rattling paper. I can't think. Since a week ago Thursday, fifty-one stolen cars have been recovered in the South and Southwest. And we don't know which two, if any, belonged to this mob. We don't even know which route they took away from here. Believe it or not—nobody saw 'em!"

As the two specialists stared bleakly at each other, a young man of fourteen named Pink Dee was sidling inconspicuously through the shadows in the rear of Louie's Garage (Tow car service—open 24 hrs.). Pink was considered to have been the least beautiful baby, the most unprepossessing child, in Leeman, and he gave frank promise of growing up to be a rather coarse joke on the entire human race. Born with a milk-blue skin, dead-white hair, little reddish weak eyes, pipe-cleaner bones, narrow forehead, no chin, beaver teeth, a voice like an unoiled hinge, nature had made the usual compensation. His reaction time was exceptional. Plenty of more rugged and more normal children had found out that Pink Dee could hit you by the time you had the word out of your mouth. The blow came from an outsize, knobby fist at the end of a long thin arm, and he swung it with all the abandon of a bag of rocks on the end of a rope. The second important item about Pink Dee came to light when the Leeman School System started giving IQs. Pink's was higher than they were willing to admit the first time, as it did not seem proper that the only genius in Leeman should be old Homer Dee's only son. Pink caught on, and the second time he was rated he got it down into the cretin class. The third rating was ninety-nine, and everybody seemed happy with that.

At fourteen Pink was six feet tall and weighed a hundred and twenty pounds. He peered at the world through heavy lenses and maintained, in the back room of his home on Fountain Street, myriad items of apparatus, some made, some purchased. There he investigated certain electrical and magnetic phenomena, having tired of building radios, and carried on a fairly virulent correspondence on the quantum theory with a Cal Tech professor who was under the impression that he was arguing with someone of more mature years.

Dressed in his khakis, Pink moved through the shadows, inserted the key he had filched into the Buick door, and then into the ignition lock. He turned it to the left to activate the electrical gimmicks, and then turned on the car radio. As soon as it warmed up, he pushed the selective buttons, carefully noting the dial. When he had the readings, he turned it to WLEE to check the accuracy of the dial. When WLEE roared into a farm report, Louie appeared and dragged Pink out by the thin scruff of his neck.

"What the hell?" Louie said.

Being unable to think of any adequate explanation, Pink wriggled away and loped out.

Pink's next stop was WLEE, where he was well known. He found the manual he wanted and spent the next twenty minutes leafing through it.

Having been subjected to a certain amount of sarcasm from both Sternweister and Weed, Hod Abrams and Lefty Quinn were in no mood for the approach Pink Dee used.

"I demand to see the FBI," Pink said firmly, the effect spoiled a bit by the fact that his voice change was so recent that the final syllable was a reversion to his childhood squeaky-hinge voice.

"He demands," Hod said to Lefty.

"Go away, Pink," Lefty growled, "before I stomp on your glasses."

"I am a citizen who wishes to speak to a member of a federal agency," Pink said with dignity.

"A citizen, maybe. A taxpayer, no. You give me trouble, kid, and I'm going to warm your pants right here in this lobby."

Maybe the potential indignity did it. Pink darted for the stairs leading up from the lobby. Hod went roaring up the stairs after him, and Lefty grabbed the elevator. They both snared him outside Sternweister's suite and found that they had a job on their hands. Pink bucked and contorted like a picnic on which a hornet's nest had just fallen.

The door to the suite opened and both Sternweister and Weed glared out, their mouths open.

"Just . . . just a fresh . . . kid," Hod Abrams panted.

"I know where the crooks are!" Pink screamed.

"He's nuts," Lefty yelled.

"Wait a minute," Randolph Sternweister ordered sharply. They stopped dragging Pink but still clung to him. "I admit he doesn't look as though he knew his way home, but you can't tell. You two wait outside. Come in here, young man."

Pink marched erectly into the suite, selected the most comfortable chair, and sank into it, looking very smug.

"Where are they?"

"Well, I don't know exactly—"

"Outside!" Weed said with a thumb motion.

"—but I know how to find out."

"Oh, you know how to find out, eh? Keep talking. I haven't laughed in nine days," Sternweister said.

"Oh, I had to do a little checking first," Pink said in a lofty manner. "I stole the key to the Buick and got into it to test something."

"Kid, experts have been over that car, half-inch by half-inch."

"Please don't interrupt me, sir. And don't take that attitude. Because if it turns out I have something, and I know I have, you're going to look as silly as anything."

Sternweister flushed and then turned pale. He held hard to the edge of a table. "Go ahead," he said thickly.

"I am making an assumption that the people who robbed our bank started out from some hide-out and then went back to the same one. I am further assuming that they were in their hide-out some time—that is, while they were planning the robbery."

Weed and Sternweister exchanged glances. "Go on."

"So my plan has certain possible flaws based on these assumptions, but at least it uncovers one possible pattern of investigation. I know that the car was stolen from Chapel Hill. That was in the paper. And I know the dead man was in Chicago. So I checked Chicago and Chapel Hill a little while ago."

"Checked them?"

"At the radio station, of course. Modern car radios are easy to set to new stations by altering the push buttons. The current settings of the push buttons do not conform either to the Chicago or the Chapel Hill areas. There are six stations that the radio in the Buick is set for, and—"

Sternweister sat down on the couch as though somebody had clubbed him behind the knees, "Agh!" he said.

"So all you have to do," Pink said calmly, "is to check areas against the push-button settings until you find an area *where all six frequencies are represented by radio stations in the immediate geographical vicinity.* It will take a bit of statistical work, of course, and a map of the country, and a supply of push pins should simplify things, I would imagine. Then, after the area is located, I would take the Buick there, and due to variations in individual sets and receiving conditions, you might be able to narrow it down to within a mile or two. Then, by showing the photograph of the dead gangster around at bars and such places—"

And that was why, on the following Wednesday, a repainted Buick with new plates and containing two agents of the Bureau roamed through the small towns near Tampa on the West Florida Coast, and how they found that the car radio in the repainted Buick brought in Tampa, Clearwater, St. Pete, Orlando, Winter Haven, and Dunedin on the push buttons with remarkable clarity the closer they came to a little resort town called Tarpon Springs. On Thursday morning at four, the portable floodlights bathed three beach cottages in a white glare, and the metallic voice of the P.A. system said, "You are surrounded. Come out with your hands high. You are surrounded."

The shots, a few moments later, cracked with a thin bitterness against the heavier sighing of the Gulf of Mexico. Mr. Stanley Woods, or, as the blonde later stated, Mr. Grebbs Fainstock, was shot, with poetic justice, through the head, and that was the end of resistance.

On Pink Dee Day in Leeman, the president of the Leeman National Bank turned over the envelope containing the reward. It came to a bit less than 6 per cent of the recovered funds, and it is ample to guarantee, at some later date, a Cal Tech degree.

In December the Sternweisters bought a new car. When Claire demanded to know why Randolph insisted on delivery *sans* car radio, his only answer was a hollow laugh.

She feels that he has probably been working too hard.

C. HEDLEY BARKER

. . . was born in a small village in Yorkshire, England. At school he found the rigors of Latin, French and German too much for him, and at the age of twelve, ran away to sea. This was a short-lived adventure, for he was caught within a few days and returned home. Eventually he did join the Navy and served on a destroyer in World War 1.

In 1919, having left the Navy, he turned to writing, and in his first years collected an impressive number of rejection slips. His first story was published in 1922, and since then, he has turned out some 500 magazine stories and about 20 novels.

Hedley Barker's gift for combining taut, dramatic action with a swift and surprising climax is shown to perfect effect in "The Ace of Trouble."

THE ACE OF TROUBLE

IT MUST have been unbearable for Herbert Dawlish to reflect that, had the waitress not been slow, he would never have committed murder.

Dawlish had just ten minutes to spare, and he was feeling infernally hungry. So he dropped into a lunch counter and called for a cup of tea and pastry. The waitress dawdled, and Herbert Dawlish fidgeted impatiently. He must have taken out his watch at least ten times in five minutes. When at last his order arrived, he had two minutes in which to bolt it down and catch the train for Herne Bay.

He rushed on to the platform just as the train was pulling out. His lips tightened with annoyance as he realized that he couldn't possibly reach the saloon as this was not a corridor train. This meant that he would miss the regular commuters and his game of cards.

The train gathered speed. Dawlish gripped his bag and ran, realizing that he would be lucky now to catch it at all. However, he managed with a flying leap to land on the footboard of the rear coach amid the yells of railway officials. He clung there for a moment, panting, then opened the door and subsided with a gasp on the seat.

The man opposite Herbert Dawlish was a flashy sort of person with a gold horseshoe in his tie, and aggressively square shoes. He said the usual things that people do say on these occasions—narrow shave, not so easy to run at Dawlish's time of life, and so forth. He also launched into a protracted and lurid reminiscence which had to do with one Sam Biggs, who being denied the luck which had attended Mr. Dawlish, fell between the footboard and the platform. To these remarks, he added a macabre postscript:

" 'Orrible sight. I never want to see another like it."

Herbert Dawlish, far as distant Jupiter in that moment from murderous intent, gazed upon the man he was going to murder. He never suffered fools gladly, and this fellow seemed a particularly vacuous specimen. However, when the man suggested a game of cards, Dawlish brightened considerably. He had a passion for cards, and he fell in eagerly with the proposal.

"I have a pack here," he said, diving into his pocket. There his fingers came in contact with something hard, and he pulled it out with an embarrassed smile. He said, jocularly, laying an automatic pistol on the table:

"Don't be alarmed. I'm no gunman. I bought this in town today. You see, I belong to the Herne Bay rifle club, and they've just started a revolver class. Fascinating sport."

The other nodded.

"May I?" he said, and, picking up the weapon, examined it with the eye of an expert. "Dandy little gun," was his comment. "Loaded, too, by gosh!"

"Er—yes. I brought some cartridges along. It's quite safe. The catch is on. Now, what shall we play? Do you happen to know Soixante-six? It's an ideal game for two."

"Swa—?"

"In other words, sixty-six. It's a kind of—"

"Right, governor! I got you. Sixty-six. Yes. Used to play it over in France. I remember during the war—"

"Cut, will you?"

Herbert Dawlish dealt.

"What about stakes?" he murmured with a swift, appraising glance at the other's ensemble.

"Oh, five shillings a time."

Dawlish was surprised. This was a good deal higher than he was used to, but he guessed he could hold his own, anyway. He dealt the cards in bundles of three and two. Play began.

Now, it very soon became obvious to Dawlish that this fellow with the horseshoe had handled cards before. He had that nifty method of shuffling and deal-

ing which involves a flourishing and crackling of the
cards. He licked his thumbs. The pasteboards flew
from his nimble fingers like greased lightning.

Dawlish paid out. Five—ten—fifteen—thirty-five—
fifty. He lost six pounds. A dull flush tinted his high
cheekbones. He fortified himself with a long pull from
his pocket flask, clenched his teeth, and concentrated
grimly.

Long before the train had reached Chatham, that six
pounds had become forty-six. Dawlish was plunging
madly to retrieve his losses. A ghastly fear contracted
his heart. He had lost much—very much more than he
could afford to lose. It was quarter day, his rent was
due, and he had calls to meet which must be met out
of this money that he was losing.

At seventy pounds Herbert Dawlish leant back and
wiped the sweat from his forehead with a shaky hand.
He was pale, and the corners of his mouth were out
of his control. A very unpleasant sight, indeed.

"I am afraid," he muttered, "that I can't go on. I've
lost every penny."

The nifty man stopped short in the midst of a tune
he was whistling. He looked at Dawlish, full square.

"That a fact?" he remarked. "Hard luck, mate.
Good game, though, eh? 'Ammer and tongs."

"Look here," said Dawlish abjectly. "I—it's a queer
thing to ask, but—could you let me have that money
back? For a little while, I mean. I would repay you,
later. But, just now, I—I—"

The nifty man had been staring at Dawlish in blank

surprise. Now he suddenly guffawed.

"Well, that's rich," he observed. "I'll tell the missus that when I gits 'ome. She'll cry 'er eyes out, that she will. No matey. Nothing doing. I ain't the Salvation Army 'Ome."

"Let me explain," begged Dawlish in agony. "You don't understand. It's like this—"

"Aw, shove a boot in it, ole feller. You oughtn't never to 'ave come out without yer nurse. Hey! What the—"

"Put up your hands," said Dawlish, staring wickedly from behind his automatic. "Right up!"

Even then, Dawlish had no notion of murder. He merely wanted to scare the fellow into parting with the money. He was frantic. He positively daren't go home and face his wife with a story of seventy pounds lost. But, firearms are dangerous things to play with. The nifty man's eyes narrowed. He made a sudden spring. And Dawlish, closing his eyes, pulled the trigger.

Death is shockingly quick and sudden. In one brief second Dawlish was saddled with a corpse. There was a grim blue hole in the middle of its forehead, and it had sagged slackly on the floor like a sack of something. Dawlish commanded himself with an effort, and began to think out ways and means.

He was about to bundle the body out of the carriage on to the railway tracks when he caught sight of a wristwatch. An inspiration caused him to alter the time of this watch to five-fifty. He counted on the watch stopping when the crash came, and a watch

stopped at five-fifty (unless the body were found immediately) would point to the fact of the man's having
traveled down by an earlier train.

This done, he opened the carriage door, looked cautiously ahead and behind; then with the train doing
about forty, shoved out the remains of the nifty man.

Venner, the Scotland Yard man, was in the eight-
forty to town on the following morning. He and two
others greeted Dawlish with ribald cries, as usual.
These four had played cards on the up journey every
day (barring holidays) for ten years. "Come along,
you old blighter—the cards," they cried. "Where were
you loafing last night, by the way?"

"Late," said Dawlish. "Had to run for it. Seen the
paper? This murder on the five-ten?"

Smith, who was sorting out Dawlish's cards, nodded.

"Poor devil's all bashed about," he said. "Face practically gone, they say. Not that he'd feel that, I suppose. You heard anything about it, Venner, apart from
what the papers give?"

Venner smiled quietly.

"I hear a good deal," he said, "that I'm not allowed
to tell. As a matter of fact, I viewed the body about
two or three hours after the murder. They rushed me
up by car from Herne Bay."

"I say," said Smith, "look here, old Dawlish, you've
only got half a pack here. The ace of trouble's missing."

Smith always called the ace of spades the ace of
trouble, because spades stood for trouble in the for-
tune-teller's jargon.

"I expect it's in my pocket," said Dawlish.

But he was spared the trouble of searching by Venner. The man from the Yard looked suddenly grave as he pulled out a card from his own pocket.

"No," he said. "Here it is, unless I'm mistaken."

He laid the ace of spades on the table—the ace which had been missing from the same pack.

"Yes, that's it, by Jove!" cried Smith. "Where the devil did you get it, you old card sharper?"

Venner turned and looked at Dawlish. Then he laid a hand on his arm.

"Dawlish," he said, "this hurts like blazes. But I've got to do it. You're arrested. That ace of spades was found up the sleeve of the murdered man."

SIR ARTHUR CONAN DOYLE

. . . was born in Edinburgh in 1859, and like many another famous writer, started his career as a doctor. As a medical student at Edinburgh University, he was deeply impressed by one of his professors, a thin, wiry and very skillful surgeon. This doctor could not only diagnose illness, but also his patients' occupations and character. Later, when Doyle started writing stories to supplement his poor medical practice, he drew on his memories of this doctor and created Sherlock Holmes —the greatest fictional detective in all literature.

In the adventure of "The Five Pips" Holmes exhibits his unusual powers of analysis and deduction. This story is considered one of Doyle's best detective stories and has attained classic status.

Revenge was the riddle concealed in

THE FIVE ORANGE PIPS

ONE OF THE most singular cases which Sherlock Holmes was called upon to solve first came to light during the latter days of September, when the equinoctial gales had set in with exceptional violence. All day the wind had screamed and the rain had beaten against the windows, so that even here in the heart of great, hand-made London we were forced to recognize the presence of those great elemental forces which shriek at mankind through the bars of his civilization, like untamed beasts in a cage.

As evening drew in, the storm grew higher and louder, and the wind cried and sobbed like a child in the chimney. Sherlock Holmes sat moodily at one side of the fireplace cross-indexing his records of crime, while I, at the other, was deep in one of Clark Russell's fine sea stories, until the howl of the gale from without seemed to blend with the text, and the splash of the rain to lengthen out into the long swash of the sea waves. My wife was on a visit to her mother's and for a few days I was a dweller once more in my old quarters at Baker Street.

"Why," said I, glancing up at my companion, "that was surely the bell. Who would come tonight? Some friend of yours, perhaps?"

"Except yourself I have none," he answered. "I do not encourage visitors."

"A client, then?"

"If so, it is a serious case. Nothing less would bring a man out on such a day and at such an hour. But I take it that it is more likely to be some crony of the land-lady's."

Sherlock Holmes was wrong in his conjecture, how-ever, for there came a step in the passage and a tapping at the door. He stretched out his long arm to turn the lamp away from himself and toward the vacant chair upon which a newcomer must sit. "Come in!" said he.

The man who entered was young, some two-and-twenty at the outside, well-groomed and trimly clad, with something of refinement and delicacy in his bear-ing. The streaming umbrella which he held in his hand, and his long shining waterproof told of the fierce weather through which he had come. He looked about him anxiously in the glare of the lamp, and I could see that his face was pale and his eyes heavy, like those of a man who is weighed down with some great anxiety.

"I owe you an apology," he said, raising his golden pince-nez to his eyes. "I trust that I am not intruding. I fear that I have brought some traces of the storm and rain into your snug chamber."

"Give me your coat and umbrella," said Holmes. "They may rest here on the hook and will be dry presently. You have come up from the southwest, I see."

"Yes, from Horsham."

"That clay and chalk mixture which I see upon your toecaps is quite distinctive."

"I have come for advice, Mr. Holmes. I heard from Major Prendergast how you saved him in the Tankerville Club scandal."

"I beg that you will draw your chair up to the fire and favor me with some details as to your case."

"It is no ordinary one."

"None of those which come to me are. Pray give us the essential facts from the commencement, and I can afterward question you as to those details which seem to me to be most important."

The young man pulled his chair up and pushed his wet feet out toward the blaze.

"My name," said he, "is John Openshaw, but my own affairs have, as far as I can understand it, little to do with this awful business. It is a hereditary matter; so in order to give you an idea of the facts, I must go back to the commencement of the affair.

"You must know that my grandfather had two sons —my uncle Elias and my father Joseph. My father had a small factory at Coventry, which he enlarged at the time of the invention of bicycling. He was a patentee of the Openshaw unbreakable tire, and his business met with such success that he was able to sell it and to retire upon a handsome competence.

"My uncle Elias emigrated to America when he was a young man and became a planter in Florida, where he was reported to have done very well. At the time of the war he fought in Jackson's army, and afterwards under Hood, where he rose to be a colonel. When Lee laid down his arms my uncle returned to his plantation, where he remained for three or four years.

"About 1869 or 1870 he came back to Europe and took a small estate in Sussex, near Horsham. He had made a very considerable fortune in the States, and his reason for leaving them was his aversion to the Negroes, and his dislike of the Republican policy in extending the franchise to them. He was a singular man, fierce and quick-tempered, very foul-mouthed when he was angry, and of a most retiring disposition.

"During all the years that he lived at Horsham, I doubt if ever he set foot in the town. He had a garden and two or three fields round his house, and there he would take his exercise, though very often for weeks on end he would never leave his room. He drank a great deal of brandy and smoked very heavily, but he would see no society and did not want any friends, not even his own brother.

"He didn't mind me; in fact, he took a fancy to me, for at the time when he saw me first I was a youngster of twelve or so. This would be in the year 1878, after he had been eight or nine years in England. He begged my father to let me live with him, and he was very kind to me in his way.

"When he was sober he used to be fond of playing backgammon and draughts with me, and he would make me his representative both with the servants and with the tradespeople, so that by the time that I was sixteen I was quite master of the house. I kept all the keys and could go where I liked and do what I liked, so long as I did not disturb him in his privacy.

"There was one singular exception, however, for he had a single room, a lumber room up among the attics, which was invariably locked, and which he would never permit either me or anyone else to enter. With a boy's curiosity I have peeped through the keyhole, but I was never able to see more than a collection of old trunks and bundles such as would be expected in such a room.

"One day—it was in March, 1883—a letter with a foreign stamp lay upon the table in front of the colonel's plate. It was not a common thing for him to receive letters, for his bills were all paid in ready money, and he had no friends of any sort. 'From India!' said he, 'Pondicherry postmark! What can this be?'

"He opened it hurriedly and out jumped five little dried orange pips, which pattered down upon his plate. I began to laugh at this, but the laugh was struck from

my lips at the sight of his face. His lip had fallen, his
eyes were protruding, his skin the color of putty, and
he glared at the envelope which he still held in his
trembling hand. "K.K.K.!" he shrieked, and then, "My
God, my God, my sins have overtaken me!'

" 'What is it, Uncle?' I cried.

" 'Death,' said he, and rising from the table he retired to his room, leaving me palpitating with horror.
I took up the envelope and saw scrawled in red ink
upon the inner flap, just above the gum, the letter K
three times repeated. There was nothing else save the
five dried pips. What could be the reason of his overpowering terror?

"I left the breakfast table, and as I ascended the
stairs I met him coming down with an old rusty key,
which must have belonged to the attic, in one hand,
and a small brass box, like a cashbox, in the other.

" 'They may do what they like, but I'll checkmate
them still,' said he with an oath. 'Tell Mary that I shall
want a fire in my room today, and send for Fordham,
the Horsham lawyer.'

"I did as he ordered, and when the lawyer arrived I
was asked to step up to the room. The fire was burning
brightly, and in the grate there was a mass of black,
fluffy ashes, as of burned paper, while the brass box
stood open and empty beside it. As I glanced at the box
I noticed, with a start, that upon the lid was printed
the treble K which I had read in the morning upon the
envelope.

" 'I wish you, John,' said my uncle, to witness my

will. I leave my estate, with all its advantages and all its disadvantages, to my brother, your father, whence it will, no doubt, descend to you. If you can enjoy it in peace, well and good! If you find you cannot, take my advice, my boy, and leave it to your deadliest enemy. I am sorry to give you such a two-edged thing, but I can't say what turn things are going to take. Kindly sign the paper where Mr. Fordham shows you.'

"I signed the paper as directed, and the lawyer took it away with him. The singular incident made, as you may think, the deepest impression upon me, and I pondered over it and turned it every way in my mind without being able to make anything of it. Yet I could not shake off the vague feeling of dread which it left behind, though the sensation grew less keen as the weeks passed, and nothing happened to disturb the usual routine of our lives.

"I could see a change in my uncle, however. He drank more than ever, and he was less inclined for any sort of society. Most of his time he would spend in his room, with the door locked upon the inside, but sometimes he would emerge in a sort of drunken frenzy and would burst out of the house and tear about the garden with a revolver in his hand, screaming out that he was afraid of no man, and that he was not to be cooped up, like a sheep in a pen, by man or devil.

"When these hot fits were over, however, he would rush tumultuously in at the door and lock and bar it behind him, like a man who can brazen it out no longer against the terror which lies at the roots of his soul. At such times I have seen his face, even on a cold day, glisten with moisture, as though it were new raised from a basin.

"Well, to come to an end of the matter, Mr. Holmes, and not to abuse your patience, there came a night when he made one of those drunken sallies from which he never came back. We found him, when we went to search for him, face downward in a little green-scummed pool, which lay at the foot of the garden. There was no sign of any violence, and the water was but two feet deep, so that the jury, having regard to his known eccentricity, brought in a verdict of suicide.

"But I, who knew how he winced from the very thought of death, had much ado to persuade myself that he had gone out of his way to meet it. The matter passed, however, and my father entered into possession of the estate, and of some £14,000, which lay to his credit at the bank."

"One moment," Holmes interposed. "Your statement is, I foresee, one of the most remarkable to which I have ever listened. Let me have the date of the reception by your uncle of the letter, and the date of his supposed suicide."

"The letter arrived on March 10, 1883. His death was seven weeks later, upon the night of May second."

"Thank you. Pray proceed."

"When my father took over the Horsham property, he, at my request, made a careful examination of the attic, which had been always locked up. We found the brass box there, although its contents had been destroyed. On the inside of the cover was a paper label, with the initials of K.K.K. repeated upon it, and 'Letters, memoranda, receipts, and a register' written beneath. These, we presume, indicated the nature of the papers which had been destroyed by Colonel Openshaw.

"For the rest, there was nothing of much importance in the attic save a great many scattered papers and notebooks bearing upon my uncle's life in America. Some of them were of the wartime and showed that he had done his duty well and had borne the repute of a brave soldier. Others were of a date during the reconstruction of the Southern states, and were mostly concerned with politics, for he had evidently taken a strong part in opposing the carpet-bag politicians who had been sent down from the North.

"Well, it was the beginning of '84 when my father came to live at Horsham, and all went as well as possible with us until the January of '85. On the fourth day after the New Year I heard my father give a sharp cry of surprise as we sat together at the breakfast table. There he was, sitting with a newly opened envelope in one hand and five dried orange pips in the outstretched palm of the other one. He had always laughed at what he called my cock-and-bull story about the colonel, but he looked very scared and puzzled now that the same thing had come upon himself.

"'Why, what on earth does this mean, John?' he stammered.

"My heart had turned to lead. 'It is K.K.K.,' said I.

"He looked inside the envelope. 'So it is,' he cried. 'Here are the very letters. But what is this, written above them?'

"'Put the papers on the sundial,' I read, peeping over his shoulder.

"'What papers? What sundial?' he asked.

"'The sundial in the garden. There is no other,' said I; "but the papers must be those that were destroyed."

"'Pooh!' said he, gripping hard at his courage. 'We are in a civilized land here, and we can't have tom-foolery of this kind. Where does the thing come from?'

"'From Dundee,' I answered, glancing at the post-mark.

"'Some preposterous practical joke,' said he. 'What have I to do with sundials and papers? I shall take no notice of such nonsense.'

"'I should certainly speak to the police,' I said.

"'No, I forbid you. I won't have a fuss made about such nonsense.'

"It was in vain to argue with him, for he was a very obstinate man. I went about, however, with a heart which was full of foreboding.

"On the third day after the coming of the letter my father went from home to visit an old friend of his, Major Freebody, who is in command of one of the forts upon Portsdown Hill. I was glad that he should go, for it seemed to me that he was farther from danger when he was away from home. In that, how-ever, I was in error. Upon the second day of his ab-sence I received a telegram from the major, imploring me to come at once.

"My father had fallen over one of the deep chalk pits which abound in the neighborhood, and was lying senseless, with a shattered skull. I hurried to him, but he died without ever having recovered consciousness. He had, as it appears, been returning from Fareham in the twilight, and as the country was unknown to him, and the chalk pit unfenced, the jury had no hesitation in bringing in a verdict of death from accidental causes.

"Carefully as I examined every fact connected with his death, I was unable to find anything which could suggest the idea of murder. There were no signs of violence, no footmarks, no robbery, no record of strangers having been seen upon the roads. And yet I need not tell you that my mind was far from at ease, and that I was well-nigh certain that some foul plot had been woven around him.

"It was in January, '85, that my poor father met his end, and two years and eight months have elapsed since then. During that time I have lived happily at Horsham, and I had begun to hope that this curse had passed away from the family, and that it had ended with the last generation. I had begun to take comfort too soon, however; yesterday morning the blow fell in the very shape in which it had come upon my father."

The young man took from his waistcoat a crumpled envelope, and turning to the table he shook out upon it five little dried orange pips.

"This is the envelope," he continued. "The postmark is London—eastern division. Within are the very words which were upon my father's last message: 'K.K.K.'; and then 'Put the papers on the sundial.' "

"What have you done?" asked Holmes.

"Nothing."

"Nothing?"

"To tell the truth"—he sank his face into his thin, white hands—"I have felt helpless. I have felt like one of those poor rabbits when the snake is writhing toward it. I seem to be in the grasp of some resistless, inexorable evil, which no foresight and no precautions can guard against."

"Tut! tut!" cried Sherlock Holmes. "You must act, man, or you are lost. Nothing but energy can save you. This is no time for despair."

"I have seen the police."

"Ah!"

"But they listened to my story with a smile. I am convinced that the inspector has formed the opinion that the letters are all practical jokes, and that the deaths of my relations were really accidents, as the jury stated, and were not to be connected with the warnings."

Holmes shook his clenched hands in the air. "Incredible imbecility!" he cried.

"They have, however, allowed me a policeman, who may remain in the house with me."

"Has he come with you tonight?"

"No. His orders were to stay in the house."

Again Holmes raved in the air.

"Why did you come to me," he cried, "and, above all, why did you not come at once?"

"I did not know. It was only today that I spoke to Major Prendergast about my troubles and was advised by him to come to you," explained the young man.

"It is really two days since you had the letter. We should have acted before this. You have no further evidence—no suggestive detail which might help us?"

"There is one thing," said John Openshaw. He rummaged in his coat pocket, and, drawing out a piece of blue-tinted paper, he laid it out upon the table.

"I have some remembrance," said he, "that on the day when my uncle burned the papers I observed that the small, unburned margins which lay amid the ashes were of this particular color. I found this single sheet upon the floor of his room, and I am inclined to think that it may be one of the papers which might, perhaps, have fluttered out from among the others, and in that way escaped destruction. Beyond the mention of pips, I do not see that it helps us much. I think myself that it is a page from some private diary. The writing is undoubtedly my uncle's."

Holmes moved the lamp, and we both bent over the sheet of paper, which showed by its ragged edge that it had indeed been torn from a book. It was headed, "March, 1869," and beneath were the following enigmatical notices:

4th. Hudson came. Same old platform.

7th. Set the pips on McCauley, Paramore, and John Swain, of St. Augustine.

9th. McCauley cleared.

10th.   John Swain cleared.
12th.   Visited Paramore. All well.

"Thank you!" said Holmes, folding up the paper and returning it to our visitor. "And now you must on no account lose another instant. We cannot spare time even to discuss what you have told me. You must get home instantly and act."

"What shall I do?"

"There is but one thing to do. It must be done at once. You must put this piece of paper which you have shown us into the brass box which you have described. You must also put in a note to say that all the other papers were burned by your uncle, and that this is the only one which remains. You must assert this in such words as will carry conviction with them. Having done that, you must at once put the box out upon the sundial, as directed. Do you understand?"

"Entirely."

"Do not think of revenge, or anything of the sort, at present. I think that we may gain that by means of the law; but we have our web to weave, while theirs is already woven. The first consideration is to remove the pressing danger which threatens you. The second is to clear up the mystery and to punish the guilty parties."

"I thank you," said the young man, rising and pulling on his overcoat. "You have given me fresh life and hope. I shall certainly do as you advise."

"Do not lose an instant. And, above all, take care of yourself in the meanwhile, for I do not think that there

can be a doubt that you are threatened by a very real
and imminent danger. How do you go back?"

"By train from Waterloo."

"It is not yet nine. The streets will be crowded, so I
trust that you may be in safety. And yet you cannot
guard yourself too closely."

"I am armed."

"That is well. Tomorrow I shall set to work upon
your case."

"I shall see you at Horsham, then?"

"No, your secret lies in London. It is there that I
shall seek it."

"Then I shall call upon you in a day, or in two days,
with news as to the box and the papers. I shall take
your advice in every particular." He shook hands with
us and took his leave. Outside the wind still screamed
and the rain splashed and pattered against the windows. This strange, wild story seemed to have come to
us from amid the mad elements—blown in upon us like
a sheet of seaweed in a gale—and now to have been re-
absorbed by them once more.

Sherlock Holmes sat for some time in silence, with
his head sunk forward and his eyes bent upon the red
glow of the fire. Then he lit his pipe, and leaning back
in his chair he watched the blue smoke rings as they
chased each other up to the ceiling.

"I think, Watson," he remarked at last, "that of all
our cases we have had none more fantastic than this."

"Save, perhaps, the Sign of the Four."

"Well, yes. Save, perhaps, that. And yet this John

Openshaw seems to me to be walking amid even greater perils than did the Sholtos."

"But have you," I asked, "formed any definite conception as to what these perils are?"

"There can be no question as to their nature," he answered.

"Then what are they? Who is this K.K.K., and why does he pursue this unhappy family?"

Sherlock Holmes closed his eyes and placed his elbows upon the arms of his chair, with his fingertips together. "The ideal reasoner," he remarked, "would, when he had once been shown a single fact in all its bearings, deduce from it not only all the chain of events which led up to it, but also the results which would follow from it. A man should keep his little brain attic stocked with all the furniture that he is likely to use, and the rest he can put away in the lumber room of his library, where he can get it if he wants it. Now, kindly hand me down the letter K of the American Encyclopaedia which stands upon the shelf beside you. Thank you.

"Now let us consider the situation and see what may be deduced from it. In the first place, we may start with a strong presumption that Colonel Openshaw had some very strong reason for leaving America. Men at his time of life do not change all their habits and exchange willingly the charming climate of Florida for the lonely life of an English provincial town. His extreme love of solitude in England suggests the idea that he was in fear of someone or something, so we may assume as a working hypothesis that it was fear of someone or something which drove him from America.

"As to what it was he feared, we can only deduce that by considering the formidable letters which were received by himself and his successors. Did you remark the postmarks of those letters?"

"The first was from Pondicherry, the second from Dundee, and the third from London."

"From East London. What do you deduce from that?"

"They are all seaports. That the writer was on board a ship."

"Excellent. We already have a clue. There can be no doubt that the probability—the strong probability—is that the writer was on board a ship. And now let us consider another point. In the case of Pondicherry, seven weeks elapsed between the threat and its fulfill-ment, in the case of Dundee it was only some three or four days. Does that suggest anything?"

"A greater distance to travel."

"But the letter had also a greater distance to come."

"Then I do not see the point."

"There is at least a presumption that the vessel in which the man or men are, is a sailing ship. It looks as if they always sent their singular warning or token be-fore them when starting upon their mission. You see how quickly the deed followed the sign when it came from Dundee. If they had come from Pondicherry in a steamer they would have arrived almost as soon as their letter. But, as a matter of fact, seven weeks elapsed. I think that those seven weeks represented the difference between the mailboat which brought the letter and the sailing vessel which brought the writer."

"It is possible."

"More than that — it is probable. And now see you the deadly urgency of this new case, and why I urged young Openshaw to caution. The blow has always fallen at the end of the time which it would take the senders to travel the distance. But this one comes from London, and therefore we cannot count upon delay."

"Good God!" I cried. "What can it mean, this relentless persecution?"

"The papers which Openshaw carried are obviously of vital importance to the person or persons in the sailing ship. I think that it is quite clear that there must be more than one of them. A single man could not have carried out two deaths in such a way as to deceive a coroner's jury. There must have been several in it, and they must have been men of resource and determination. Their papers they mean to have—be the holder of them who it may. In this way you see K.K.K. ceases to be the initials of an individual and becomes the badge of a society," Holmes expounded

"But of what society?"

"Have you never—" said Sherlock Holmes, bending forward and sinking his voice— "have you never heard of the Ku Klux Klan?"

"I never have."

Holmes turned over the leaves of the book upon his knee. "Here it is," said he presently:

Ku Klux Klan. A name derived from the fanciful resemblance to the sound produced by cocking a rifle. This terrible secret society was formed by some ex-Confederate soldiers in the Southern states after the Civil War, and it rapidly formed local branches in different parts of the country, notably in Tennessee, Louisiana, the Carolinas, Georgia, and Florida.

Its power was used for political purposes, principally for the terrorizing of the Negro voters and the murdering and driving from the country of those who were opposed to its views. Its outrages were usually preceded by a warning sent to the marked man in some fantastic but generally recognized shape—a sprig of oak leaves in some parts, melon seeds or orange pips in others.

On receiving this the victim might either openly abjure his former ways, or might fly from the country. If he braved the matter out, death would unfailingly come upon him, and usually in some strange and unforeseen manner. So perfect was the organization of the society, and so systematic its methods, that there is hardly a case upon record where any man succeeded in braving it with impunity, or in which any of its outrages were traced home to the perpetrators.

Eventually, in 1869, the movement rather suddenly collapsed, although there have since been sporadic outbreaks.

"You will observe," said Holmes, laying down the volume, "that the sudden breaking up of the society was coincident with the disappearance of Openshaw from America with their papers. It may well have been cause and effect. It is no wonder that he and his family have some of the more implacable spirits upon their track. You can understand that this register and diary may implicate some of the first men in the South, and that there may be many who will not sleep easy at night until it is recovered."

"Then the page we have seen——"

"Is such as we might expect. It ran, if I remember

right, 'sent the pips to A, B, and C'—that is, sent the society's warning to them. Then there are successive entries that A and B cleared, or left the country, and finally that C was visited, with, I fear, a sinister result for C. Well, I think, Doctor, that we may let some light into this dark place, and I believe that the only chance young Openshaw has in the meantime is to do what I have told him. There is nothing more to be said or to be done tonight, so hand me over my violin and let us try to forget for half an hour the miserable weather and the still more miserable ways of our fellowmen."

It had cleared in the morning, and the sun was shining with a subdued brightness through the dim veil which hangs over the great city. Sherlock Holmes was already at breakfast when I came down.

"You will excuse me for not waiting for you," said he, "I have, I foresee, a very busy day before me in looking into this case of young Openshaw's."

"What steps will you take?" I asked.

"It will very much depend upon the results of my first inquiries. I may have to go down to Horsham, after all."

"You will not go there first?"

"No, I shall commence with the City. Just ring the bell and the maid will bring up your coffee."

As I waited, I lifted the unopened newspaper from the table and glanced over it. My eye rested upon a heading which sent a chill to my heart.

"Holmes," I cried, "you are too late."

"Ah!" said he, laying down his cup, "I feared as much. How was it done?" He spoke calmly, but I could see that he was deeply moved.

"My eye caught the name of Openshaw, and the heading "Tragedy Near Waterloo Bridge." Here is the account:

Between nine and ten last night Police-Constable Cook, of the H Division, on duty near Waterloo Bridge, heard a cry for help and a splash in the water. The night, however, was extremely dark and stormy, so that, in spite of the help of several passers-by, it was quite impossible to effect a rescue.

The alarm, however, was given, and, by the aid of the river police, the body was eventually recovered. It proved to be that of a young gentleman whose name, as it appears from an envelope which was found in his pocket, was John Openshaw, and whose residence is near Horsham. It is conjectured that he may have been hurrying down to catch the last train from Waterloo Station, and that in his haste and the extreme darkness, he missed his path and walked over the edge of one of the small landing places for river steamboats.

The body exhibited no traces of violence, and there can be no doubt that the deceased had been the victim of an unfortunate accident, which should have the effect of calling the attention of the authorities to the condition of the riverside landing stages.

We sat in silence for some minutes, Holmes more depressed and shaken than I had ever seen him.

"That hurts my pride, Watson," he said at last. "It is a petty feeling, no doubt, but it hurts my pride. It becomes a personal matter with me now, and, if God sends me health, I shall set my hand upon this gang. That he should come to me for help, and that I should send him away to his death——!" He sprang from his chair and paced about the room in uncontrollable agitation, with a flush upon his sallow cheeks and a nervous clasping and unclasping of his long thin hands.

"They must be cunning devils!" he exclaimed at last. "How could they have decoyed him down there? The Embankment is not on the direct line to the station. The bridge, no doubt, was too crowded, even on such a night, for their purpose. Well, Watson, we shall see who will win in the long run. I am going out now!"

"To the police?"

"No; I shall be my own police. When I have spun the web they may take the flies, but not before."

All day I was engaged in my professional work, and it was late in the evening before I returned to Baker Street. Sherlock Holmes had not come back yet. It was nearly ten o'clock before he entered, looking pale and worn. He walked up to the sideboard, and tearing a piece of bread from the loaf he devoured it voraciously, washing it down with a long draught of water.

"You are hungry," I remarked.

"Starving. It had escaped my memory. I have had nothing since breakfast."

"And how have you succeeded?"

"Well."

"You have a clue?"

"I have them in the hollow of my hand. Young Openshaw shall not long remain unavenged. Why, Watson, let us put their own devilish trademark upon them. It is well thought of!"

"What do you mean?"

He took an orange from the cupboard, and tearing it to pieces he squeezed out the pips upon the table. Of these he took five and thrust them into an envelope. On the inside of the flap he wrote "S.H. for J.C." Then he sealed it and addressed it to "Captain James Calhoun, Bark *Lone Star,* Savannah, Georgia."

"That will await him when he enters port," said he, chuckling. "It may give him a sleepless night. He will find it as sure a precursor of his fate as Openshaw did before him."

"And who is this Captain Calhoun?"

"The leader of the gang. I shall have the others, but he is the first."

"How did you trace it, then?"

He took a large sheet of paper from his pocket, all covered with dates and names.

"I have spent the whole day," said he, "poring over Lloyd's registers and files of the old papers, following the career of every vessel which touched at Pondicherry in January and February of '83. There were thirty-six ships of fair tonnage which were reported there during those months. Of these, one, the *LONE STAR,* instantly attracted my attention, since, although it was reported as having cleared from London, the name is that which is given to one of the states of the Union."

"Texas, I think."

"I was not and am not sure which; but I knew that the ship must have an American origin."

"What then?"

"I searched the Dundee records, and when I found

that the bark *Lone Star* was there in January, '85, my suspicion became a certainty. I then inquired as to the vessels which lay at present in the Port of London."

"Yes?"

"The *Lone Star* had arrived here last week. I went down to the Albert Dock and found that she had been taken down the river by the early tide this morning, homeward bound to Savannah. I wired Gravesend and learned that she had passed some time ago."

"What will you do, then?"

"Oh, I have my hand upon him. He and the two mates, are, as I learn, the only native-born Americans aboard the ship. By the time their sailing ship reaches Savannah, the mailboat will have delivered this letter, and the cable will have informed the police of Savannah that these three gentlemen are badly wanted here upon a charge of murder."

There is ever a flaw, however, in the best laid of human plans, and the murderers of John Openshaw were never to receive the orange pips which would have shown them that another, as cunning and as resolute as themselves, was upon their track.

Very long and very severe were the equinoctial gales that year. We waited long for news of the *Lone Star* of Savannah, but none ever reached us. We did at last hear that somewhere far out in the Atlantic a shattered stern-post of the boat was seen swinging in the trough of a wave, with the letters "L. S." carved upon it, and that is all which we shall ever know of the fate of the *Lone Star*.

Sherlock Holmes discovers

THE RED-HEADED LEAGUE

is part of a fiendish plot

I HAD CALLED upon my friend, Mr. Sherlock Holmes, one day in the autumn of last year, and found him in deep conversation with a very stout, florid-faced elderly gentleman, with fiery red hair. With an apology for my intrusion, I was about to withdraw, when Holmes pulled me abruptly into the room and closed the door.

"You could not possibly have come at a better time, my dear Watson," he said, cordially.

"I was afraid that you were engaged."

"Not at all. This gentleman, Mr. Wilson, has been my partner and helper in many of my most successful cases, and I have no doubt that he will be of the utmost use to me in yours also."

The stout gentleman half rose from his chair and

gave a bob of greeting, with a quick little questioning glance from his small, fat-encircled eyes.

"Try the settee," said Holmes, relapsing into his armchair, and putting his fingertips together, as was his custom when in judicial moods. "Now, perhaps, Mr. Wilson, you would have the great kindness to recommence your narrative. I ask you, not merely because my friend, Dr. Watson, has not heard the opening part, but also because the peculiar nature of the story makes me anxious to have every possible detail from your lips.

The portly client puffed out his chest with an appearance of some little pride, and pulled a dirty and wrinkled newspaper from the inside pocket of his greatcoat. As he glanced down the advertisement column, with his head thrust forward, and the paper flattened out upon his knee, I took a good look at the man, and endeavored, after the fashion of my companion, to read the indications which might be presented by his dress or appearance.

I did not gain very much, however, by my inspection. Our visitor bore every mark of being an average commonplace British tradesman, obese, pompous, and slow-moving. Altogether, look as I would, there was nothing remarkable about the man save his blazing red head and the expression of extreme chagrin and discontent upon his features.

Sherlock Holmes's quick eye took in my occupation, and he shook his head with a smile as he noticed my questioning glances. "Beyond the obvious facts that he has at some time done manual labor, that he takes snuff, that he is a Freemason, that he has been in China, and that he has done a considerable amount of writing lately, I can deduce nothing else."

Mr. Jabez Wilson started up in his chair, with his forefinger upon the paper, but his eyes upon my companion.

"How, in the name of good fortune did you know all that, Mr. Holmes?" he asked. "How did you know, for example, that I did manual labor? It's as true as gospel, for I began as a ship's carpenter."

"Your hands, my dear sir. Your right hand is quite a size larger than your left. You have worked with it and the muscles are more developed."

"Well, the snuff, then, and the Freemasonry?"

"I won't insult your intelligence by telling you how I read that, especially as, rather against the strict rules of your order, you use an arc and compass breastpin."

"Ah, of course, I forgot that. But the writing?"

"What else can be indicated by that right cuff so very shiny for five inches, and the left one with the smooth patch near the elbow where you rest it upon the desk."

"Well, but China?"

"The fish which you have tattooed immediately above your wrist could only have been done in China. I have made a small study of tattoo marks, and have even contributed to the literature of the subject. The trick of staining the fishes' scales a delicate pink is quite peculiar to China. When, in addition, I see a Chinese coin hanging from your watch-chain, the matter becomes even more simple," said Holmes.

Mr. Jabez Wilson laughed heavily. "Well, I never!" said he. "I thought at first that you had done something clever, but I see that there was nothing in it after all."

"I begin to think, Watson," said Holmes, "that I make a mistake in explaining. 'Omne ignotum pro magnifico,' you know, and my poor little reputation, such as it is, will suffer shipwreck if I am so candid. Can you not find the advertisement, Mr. Wilson?"

"Here it is. This is what began it all. You just read it for yourself, sir."

I took the paper from him and read as follows:

"TO THE RED-HEADED LEAGUE: On account of the bequest of the late Ezekiah Hopkins, of Lebanon, Pa., U.S.A., there is now another vacancy open which entitles a member of the League to a salary of four pounds a week for purely nominal services. All red-headed men who are sound in body and mind and above the age of twenty-one years are eligible. Apply in person on Monday, at eleven o'clock, to Duncan Ross, at the offices of the League, 7 Pope's Court, Fleet Street."

"What on earth does this mean?" I ejaculated, after I had twice read over the extraordinary announcement.

Holmes chuckled and wriggled in his chair, as was his habit when in high spirits. "It is a little off the beaten track, isn't it?" said he. "And now, Mr. Wilson, off you go at scratch, and tell us all about yourself, your household, and the effect which this advertisement had upon your fortunes. You will first make a note, doctor, of the paper and the date."

"It is *The Morning Chronicle* of just two months ago."

"Very good. Now, Mr. Wilson."

"Well, it is just as I have been telling you, Mr. Sherlock Holmes," said Jabez Wilson, mopping his forehead, "I have a small pawnbroker's business at Coburg Square, near the City. It's not a very large affair, and of late years it has not done more than just give me a living. I used to be able to keep two assistants, but now I only keep one, and I would have a job to pay him but that he is willing to come for half wages, so as to learn the business."

"What is the name of this obliging youth?" asked Sherlock Holmes.

"His name is Vincent Spaulding, and he's not such a youth either. It's hard to say his age. I should not wish a smarter assistant, Mr. Holmes; and I know very well that he could better himself, and earn twice what I am able to give him. But, after all, if he is satisfied, why should I put ideas in his head?"

"Why, indeed? You seem most fortunate in having an employee who comes under the full market price. It is not a common experience among employers in this age. I don't know that your assistant is not as remarkable as your advertisement."

"Oh, he has his faults, too," said Mr. Wilson. "Never was such a fellow for photography. Snapping away with a camera when he ought to be improving his mind, and then diving down into the cellar like a rabbit into its hole to develop his pictures. That is his main fault; but, on the whole, he's a good worker. There's no vice in him."

"He is still with you, I presume?"

"Yes, sir. He and a girl of fourteen, who does a bit of simple cooking, and keeps the place clean—that's all I have in the house, for I am a widower, and never had any family. We live very quietly, sir, the three of us; and we keep a roof over our heads, and pay our debts, if we do nothing more.

"The first thing that put us out was that advertisement. Spaulding, he came down into the office just this day eight weeks, with this very paper in his hand, and he says:

" 'I wish to the Lord, Mr. Wilson, that I was a red-headed man.'

" 'Why that?' I asks.

" 'Why,' says he, 'here's another vacancy on the League of the Red-headed Men. It's worth quite a little fortune to any man who gets it, and I understand that there are more vacancies than there are men, so that the trustees are at their wits' end what to do with the money. If my hair would only change color here's a nice little crib all ready for me to step into.'

" 'Why, what is it, then?' I asked. You see, Mr. Holmes, I am a very stay-at-home man, and, as my business came to me instead of my having to go to it, I was often weeks on end without putting my foot over the door-mat. In that way I didn't know much of what was going on outside, and I was always glad of a bit of news.

" 'Have you never heard of the League of the Red-headed Men?' he asked, with his eyes open.

" 'Never.'

" 'Why, I wonder at that, for you are eligible yourself for one of the vacancies.'

" 'And what are they worth?' I asked.

" 'Oh, merely a couple of hundred a year, but the work is slight, and it need not interfere very much with one's other occupations.'

"Well, you can easily think that that made me prick up my ears, for the business has not been over good for some years, and an extra couple of hundred would have been very handy.

" 'Tell me all about it,' said I.

" 'Well,' said he, showing me the advertisement, 'you can see for yourself that the League has a vacancy, and there is the address where you should apply for particulars. As far as I can make out, the League was founded by an American millionaire, Ezekiah Hopkins, who was very peculiar in his ways. He was himself red-headed, and he had a great sympathy for all red-headed men; so, when he died, it was found that he had left his enormous fortune in the hands of trustees, with instructions to apply the interest to the providing of easy berths to men whose hair is of that color. From all I hear it is splendid pay, and very little to do.'

" 'But,' said I, 'there would be millions of red-headed men who would apply.'

" 'Not so many as you might think,' he answered. 'You see it is really confined to Londoners, and to grown men. This American had started from London when he was young, and he wanted to do the old town a good turn. Then, again, I have heard it is no use your applying if your hair is light red, or dark red, or anything but real, bright, blazing, fiery red. Now, if you cared to apply, Mr. Wilson, you would just walk in; but perhaps it would hardly be worth your while to put yourself out of the way for the sake of a few hundred pounds.'

"Now it is a fact, gentlemen, as you may see for yourselves, that my hair is of a very full and rich tint, so that it seemed to me that, if there was to be any competition in the matter, I stood as good a chance as any man that I had ever met. Vincent Spaulding seemed to know so much about it that I thought he might prove useful, so I just ordered him to put up the shutters for the day, and to come right away with me. He was very willing to have a holiday, so we shut the business up, and started off for the address that was given us in the advertisement.

"I never hope to see such a sight as that again, Mr. Holmes. From north, south, east, and west every man who had a shade of red in his hair had tramped into the City to answer the advertisement. Fleet Street was choked with red-headed folk, and Pope's Court looked like a coster's orange barrow. I should not have thought there were so many in the whole country as were brought together by that single advertisement. Every shade of color they were—straw, lemon, orange, brick, Irish-setter, liver, clay; but, as Spaulding said, there were not many who had the real vivid flame-colored tint. When I saw how many were waiting, I would have given it up in despair; but Spaulding would not hear of it. How he did it I could not imagine, but he pushed and pulled and butted until he got me through the crowd, and right up to the steps which led to the office. There was a double stream upon the stair, some going up in hope, and some coming back dejected; but we wedged in as well as we could, and soon found ourselves in the office."

"Your experience has been a most entertaining one," remarked Holmes, as his client paused and refreshed his memory with a huge pinch of snuff. "Pray continue your very interesting statement."

"There was nothing in the office but a couple of wooden chairs and a deal table, behind which sat a small man, with a head that was even redder than mine. He said a few words to each candidate as he came up, and then he always managed to find some fault in them which would disqualify them. Getting a vacancy did not seem to be such a very easy matter after all. However, when our turn came, the little man was much more favorable to me than to any of the others, and he closed the door as we entered, so that he might have a private word with us.

" 'This is Mr. Jabez Wilson,' said my assistant, 'and he is willing to fill a vacancy in the League.'

" 'And he is admirably suited for it,' the other answered. 'He has every requirement. I cannot recall when I have seen anything so fine.' He took a step backward, cocked his head on one side, and gazed at my hair until I felt quite bashful. Then suddenly he plunged forward, wrung my hand, and congratulated me warmly on my success.

" 'It would be an injustice to hesitate,' said he. 'You will, however, I am sure, excuse me for taking an obvious precaution.' With that he seized my hair in both hands, and tugged until I yelled with the pain. 'There is water in your eyes,' said he, as he released me. 'I perceive that all is as it should be. But we have to be careful, for we have twice been deceived by wigs and once by paint. I could tell you tales of cobbler's wax which would disgust you with human nature.' He stepped over to the window and shouted through it at the top of his voice that the vacancy was filled. A groan of disappointment came up from below, and the folk all trooped away in different directions, until there was not a red head to be seen except my own and that of the manager.

" 'My name,' said he, 'is Mr. Duncan Ross, and I am myself one of the pensioners upon the fund left by our noble benefactor. Are you a married man, Mr. Wilson? Have you a family?'

"I answered that I had not.

"His face fell immediately.

" 'Dear me!' he said, gravely, 'that is very serious indeed. I am sorry to hear you say that. The fund was, of course, for the propagation and spread of the redheads as well as for their maintenance. It is exceedingly unfortunate that you should be a bachelor.'

"My face lengthened at this, Mr. Holmes, for I thought that I was not to have the vacancy after all; but, after thinking it over for a few minutes, he said that it would be all right.

" 'In the case of another,' said he, 'the objection might be fatal, but we must stretch a point in favor of a man with such a head of hair as yours. When shall you be able to enter upon your new duties?'

" 'Well, it is a little awkward, for I have a business already,' said I.

" 'Oh, never mind about that, Mr. Wilson!' said Vincent Spaulding. 'I shall be able to look after that for you.'

" 'What would be the hours?' I asked.

" 'Ten to two.'

"Now a pawnbroker's business is mostly done of an evening, Mr. Holmes, especially Thursday and Friday evenings, which is just before pay-day; so it would suit me very well to earn a little in the mornings. Besides, I knew that my assistant was a good man, and that he would see to anything that turned up.

" 'That would suit me very well. And the pay?'

" 'Is four pounds a week.'

" 'And the work?'

" 'Is purely nominal.'

" 'What do you call purely nominal?'

" 'Well, you have to be in the office, or at least in the building, the whole time. If you leave, you forfeit your whole position forever. The will is very clear upon that point. You don't comply with the conditions if you budge from the office during that time.'

" 'It's only four hours a day, and I should not think of leaving,' said I.

" 'No excuse will avail,' said Mr. Duncan Ross, 'neither sickness, nor business, nor anything else. There you must stay, or lose your billet.'

" 'And the work?'

" 'Is to copy out the "Encyclopaedia Britannica." There is the first volume of it in that press. You must find your own ink, pens, and blotting-paper. Will you be ready tomorrow?'

" 'Certainly,' I answered.

" 'Then, good-by, Mr. Jabez Wilson, and let me congratulate you once more on the important position which you have been fortunate enough to gain.' He bowed me out of the room, and I went home with my assistant hardly knowing what to say or do, I was so pleased at my own good fortune.

"Well, I thought over the matter all day, and by evening I was in low spirits again; for I had quite persuaded myself that the whole affair must be some great hoax or fraud, though what its object might be I could not imagine. It seemed altogether past belief that any one could make such a will, or that they would pay such a sum for doing anything so simple as copying out the 'Encyclopaedia Britannica.' Vincent Spaulding did what he could to cheer me up, but by bedtime I had reasoned myself out of the whole thing. However, in the morning I determined to have a look at it anyhow, so I bought a penny bottle of ink, and with a quill pen and seven sheets of foolscap paper I started off for Pope's Court.

"Well, to my surprise and delight everything was right as possible. The table was set out ready for me, and Mr. Duncan Ross was there to see that I got fairly to work. He started me off upon the letter A, and then he left me; but he would drop in from time to time to see that all was right with me. At two o'clock he bade me good-day, complimented me upon the amount that I had written, and locked the door of the office after me.

"This went on day after day, Mr. Holmes, and on Saturday the manager came in and planked down four golden sovereigns for my week's work. It was the same next week, and the same the week after. Every morning I was there, at ten, and every afternoon I left at two. By degrees Mr. Duncan Ross took to coming in only once of a morning, and then, after a time, he did not come in at all. Still, of course, I never dared to leave the room for an instant, for I was not sure when he might come, and the billet was such a good one, and suited me so well, that I would not risk the loss of it.

"Eight weeks passed away like this, and I had written about Abbots, and Archery, and Armor, and Architecture and Attica, and hoped with diligence that I might get on to the B's before very long. It cost me something in foolscap, and I had pretty nearly filled a shelf with my writings. And then suddenly the whole business came to an end," he exploded.

"To an end?"

"Yes, sir. And no later than this morning. I went to work as usual at ten o'clock, but the door was shut and locked, with a little square of cardboard hammered onto the middle of the panel with a tack. Here it is, and you can read for yourself."

He held up a piece of white cardboard about the size of a sheet of note-paper. It read in this fashion:

"THE RED-HEADED LEAGUE DISSOLVED.

Oct. 9, 1890."

Sherlock Holmes and I surveyed this curt announcement and the rueful face behind it, until the comical side of the affair so completely overtopped every consideration that we both burst out into a roar of laughter.

"I cannot see that there is anything very funny," cried our client, flushing up to the roots of his flaming hair. "If you can do nothing better than laugh at me, I can go elsewhere."

"No, no," cried Holmes, shoving him back into the chair from which he had half-risen. "I really wouldn't miss your case for the world. It is most refreshingly unusual. But there is, if you will excuse my saying so, something just a little funny about it. Pray what steps did you take when you found the card upon the door?"

"I was staggered, sir. I did not know what to do. Then I called round at the offices, but none of them seemed to know anything about it. Finally, I went to the landlord, who is an accountant living on the ground floor, and I asked him if he could tell me what had become of the Red-headed League. He said that he had never heard of any such body. Then I asked him who Mr. Duncan Ross was. He answered that the name was new to him.

" 'Well,' said I, 'the gentleman at No. 4.'

" 'What, the red-headed man?'

" 'Yes.'

" 'Oh,' said he, 'his name was William Morris. He was a solicitor, and was using my room as a temporary convenience until his new premises were ready. He moved out yesterday.'

" 'Where could I find him?'

" 'Oh, at his new offices. He did tell me the address. Yes, 17 King Edward Street, near St. Paul's.'

"I started off, Mr. Holmes, but when I got to that address it was a manufactory of artificial knee-caps, and no one in it had ever heard of either Mr. William Morris, or Mr. Duncan Ross."

"And what did you do then?" asked Holmes.

"I went home to Saxe-Coburg Square, and I took the advice of my assistant. But he could not help me in any way. He could only say that if I waited I should hear by post. But that was not quite good enough, Mr. Holmes. I did not wish to lose such a place without a struggle, so, as I had heard that you were good enough to give advice to poor folk who were in need of it, I came right away to you."

"And you did very wisely," said Holmes. "Your case is an exceedingly remarkable one, and I shall be happy to look into it. From what you have told me I think that it is possible that graver issues hang from it than might at first sight appear."

"Grave enough!" said Mr. Jabez Wilson. "Why, I have lost four pounds a week."

"As far as you are personally concerned," remarked Holmes, "I do not see that you have any grievance against this extraordinary league. On the contrary, you are, as I understand, richer by some thirty pounds, to say nothing of the minute knowledge which you have gained on every subject which comes under the letter A. You have lost nothing but them."

"No, sir. But I want to find out about them, and who they are, and what their object was in playing this prank—if it was a prank—upon me. It was a pretty expensive joke for them, for it cost them two-and-thirty pounds."

"We shall endeavor to clear up these points for you. And, first, one or two questions, Mr. Wilson. This assistant of yours who first called your attention to the advertisement—how long had he been with you?"

"About a month then."

"How did he come?"

"In answer to an advertisement."

"Was he the only applicant?"

"No, I had a dozen."

"Why did you pick him?"

"Because he was handy and would come cheap."

"At half wages, in fact."

"Yes."

"What is he like, this Vincent Spaulding?"

"Small, stout-built, very quick in his ways, no hair on his face, though he's not short of thirty. Has a white splash of acid upon his forehead."

Holmes sat up in his chair, in considerable excitement. "I thought as much," said he. "Have you ever observed that his ears are pierced for earrings?"

"Yes, sir. He told me that a gypsy had done it for him when he was a lad."

"Hum!" said Holmes, sinking back in deep thought. "He is still with you?"

"Oh, yes, sir; I have only just left him."

"And has your business been attended to in your absence?"

"Nothing to complain of, sir. There's never very much to do of a morning."

"That will do, Mr. Wilson. I shall be happy to give you an opinion upon the subject in the course of a day or two. To-day is Saturday, and I hope that by Monday we may come to a conclusion.

"Well, Watson," said Holmes, when our visitor had left us, "what do you make of it all?"

"I make nothing of it," I answered, frankly. "It is a most mysterious business."

"As a rule," said Holmes, "the more bizarre a thing is the less mysterious it proves to be. It is your commonplace, featureless crimes which are really puzzling, just as a commonplace face is the most difficult to identify. But I must be prompt over this matter."

"What are you going to do, then?" I asked.

"To smoke," he answered. "It is quite a three-pipe

problem, and I beg that you won't speak to me for fifty minutes." He curled himself up in his chair, with his thin knees drawn up to his hawk-like nose, and there he sat with his eyes closed and his black clay pipe thrusting out like the bill of some strange bird. I had come to the conclusion that he had dropped asleep, and indeed was nodding myself, when he suddenly sprang out of his chair with the gesture of a man who has made up his mind, and put his pipe down upon the mantelpiece.

"Sarasate plays at St. James's Hall this afternoon," he remarked. "What do you think, Watson? Could your patients spare you for a few hours?"

"I have nothing to do to-day. My practice is never very absorbing."

"Then put on your hat and come. I am going through the City first, and we can have some lunch on the way. I observe that there is a good deal of German music on the program, which is rather more to my taste than Italian or French. It is introspective, and I want to introspect. Come along!"

We traveled by the Underground as far as Aldersgate; and a short walk took us to Saxe-Coburg Square, the scene of the singular story which we had listened to in the morning. It was a poky, little, shabby-genteel place, where four lines of dingy, two-storied brick houses looked out into a small railed-in inclosure, where a lawn of weedy grass, and a few clumps of faded laurel bushes made a hard fight against a smoke-laden and uncongenial atmosphere. Three gilt balls and a brown board with JABEZ WILSON in white letters, upon a corner house, announced the place where our red-headed client carried on his business. Sherlock Holmes stopped in front of it with his head on one side, and looked it all over, with his eyes shining brightly between puckered lids. Then he walked slowly up the street, and then down again to the corner, still looking keenly at the houses. Finally he returned to the pawnbroker's and, having thumped vigorously upon the pavement with his stick two or three times, he went up to the door and knocked. It was instantly opened by a bright-looking, clean-shaven young fellow, who asked him to step in.

"Thank you," said Holmes, "I only wished to ask you how you would go from here to the Strand."

"Third right, four left," answered the assistant, promptly, closing the door.

"Smart fellow, that," observed Holmes as we walked away. "He is, in my judgment, the fourth smartest man in London, and for daring I am not sure that he has not a claim to be third. I have known something of him before."

"Evidently," said I, "Mr. Wilson's assistant counts for a good deal in this mystery of the Red-headed League. I am sure that you inquired your way merely in order that you might see him."

"Not him."

"What then?"

"The knees of his trousers."

"And what did you see?"

"What I expected to see," said Sherlock Holmes.

"Why did you beat the pavement?"

"My dear doctor, this is a time for observation, not for talk. We are spies in an enemy's country. We know something of Saxe-Coburg Square. Let us now explore the parts which lie behind it."

The road in which we found ourselves as we turned round the corner from the retired Saxe-Coburg Square presented as great a contrast to it as the front of a picture does to the back. It was one of the main arteries which convey the traffic of the City to the north and west. The roadway was blocked with the immense stream of commerce flowing in a double tide inward and outward, while the footpaths were black with the hurrying swarm of pedestrians. It was difficult to realize, as we looked at the line of fine shops and stately business premises, that they really abutted on the other side upon the faded and stagnant square which we had just quitted.

"Let me see," said Holmes, standing at the corner, and glancing along the line, "I should like just to remember the order of the houses here. It is a hobby of mine to have an exact knowledge of London. There is Mortimer's, the tobacconist; the little newspaper shop, the Coburg branch of the City and Suburban Bank, the Vegetarian Restaurant, and McFarlane's carriage-building depot. That carries us right on to the other block. And now, doctor, we've done our work, so it's time we had some play. A sandwich and a cup of coffee, and then off to violin-land, where all is sweetness, and delicacy, and harmony, and there are no red-headed clients to vex us with their conundrums."

My friend was an enthusiastic musician, being himself not only a very capable performer, but a composer of no ordinary merit. All the afternoon he sat in the stalls wrapped in the most perfect happiness, gently waving his long thin fingers in time to the music, while his gently smiling face and his languid, dreamy eyes were as unlike those of Holmes the sleuth-hound, Holmes the relentless, keen-witted, ready-handed criminal agent, as it was possible to conceive. In his singular character the dual nature alternately asserted itself, and his extreme exactness and astuteness represented, as I have often thought, the reaction against the poetic and contemplative mood which occasionally predominated in him. The swing of his nature took him from extreme languor to devouring energy; and, as I knew well, he was never so truly formidable as when, for days on end, he had been lounging in his armchair amid his improvisations and his black-letter editions. Then it was that the lust of the chase would suddenly come upon him, and that his brilliant reasoning power would rise to the level of intuition, until those who were unacquainted with his methods would look askance at him as on a man whose knowledge was not that of other mortals. When I saw him that afternoon so enwrapped in the music at St. James's Hall, I felt that an evil time might be coming upon those whom he had set himself to hunt down.

"You want to go home, no doubt, doctor," he remarked, as we emerged. He looked at me smilingly.

"Yes, it would be as well."

"And I have some business to do which will take some hours. This business at Coburg Square is serious."

"Why serious?"

"A considerable crime is in contemplation. I have every reason to believe that we shall be in time to stop it. But to-day being Saturday rather complicates matters. I shall want your help tonight."

"At what time?"

"Ten will be early enough."

"I shall be at Baker Street at ten."

"Very well. And, I say, doctor! there may be some little danger, so kindly put your army revolver in your pocket." He waved his hand, turned on his heel, and disappeared in an instant among the crowd.

I trust that I am not more dense than my neighbors, but I was always oppressed with a sense of my own stupidity in my dealings with Sherlock Holmes. Here I had heard what he had heard, I had seen what he had seen, and yet from his words it was evident that he saw clearly not only what had happened, but what was about to happen, while to me the whole business was still confused and grotesque. As I drove home to my house in Kensington I thought over it all, from the extraordinary story of the red-headed copier of the "Encyclopaedia" down to the visit to Saxe-Coburg Square, and the ominous words with which he had parted from me. What was this nocturnal expedition, and why should I go armed? Where were we going, and what were we to do? I had the hint from Holmes that this smooth-faced pawnbroker's assistant was a formidable man—a man who might play a deep game. I tried to puzzle it out, but gave it up in despair, and set the matter aside until night should bring an explanation.

It was a quarter-past nine when I started from home and made my way across the Park, and so through Oxford Street to Baker Street. Two hansoms were standing at the door, and, as I entered the passage, I heard the sound of voices from above. On entering his room, I found Holmes in animated conversation with two men, one of whom I recognized as Peter Jones, the official police agent; while the other was a long, thin, sad-faced man, with a very shiny hat and oppressively respectable frock-coat.

"Ha! our party is complete," said Holmes, buttoning up his pea-jacket, and taking his heavy hunting crop from the rack. "Watson, I think you know Mr. Jones, of Scotland Yard? Let me introduce you to Mr. Merryweather, who is to be our companion in to-night's adventure."

"We're hunting in couples again, doctor, you see," said Jones, in his consequential way. "Our friend here is a wonderful man for starting a chase. All he wants is an old dog to help him do the running down."

"I hope a wild goose may not prove to be the end of our chase," observed Mr. Merryweather, gloomily.

"You may place considerable confidence in Mr. Holmes, sir," said the police agent, loftily. "He has his own little methods, which are, if he won't mind my saying so, just a little too theoretical and fantastic, but he has the makings of a detective in him. It is not too much to say that once or twice, as in that business of the Sholto murder and the Agra treasure, he has been more nearly correct than the official force."

"Oh, if you say so, Mr. Jones, it is all right!" said the stranger with deference. "Still, I confess that I miss my rubber. It is the first Saturday night for seven-and-twenty years that I have not had my rubber."

"I think you will find," said Sherlock Holmes, "that you will play for a higher stake to-night than you have ever done yet, and the play will be more exciting. For you, Mr. Merryweather, the stake will be some thirty thousand pounds; and for you, Jones, it will be the man upon whom you wish to lay your hands."

"John Clay, the murderer, thief, smasher, and forger. He's a young man, Mr. Merryweather, but he is at the head of his profession, and I would rather have my bracelets on him than on any criminal in London. He's a remarkable man, is young John Clay. His grandfather was a Royal Duke, and he himself has been to Eton and Oxford. His brain is as cunning as his fingers, and though we meet signs of him at every turn, we never know where to find the man himself. He'll crack a crib in Scotland one week, and be raising money to build an orphanage in Cornwall the next. I've been on his track for years, and have never set eyes on him yet."

"I hope that I may have the pleasure of introducing you tonight. I've had one or two little turns also with Mr. John Clay, and I agree with you that he is at the head of his profession. It is past ten, however, and quite time that we started. If you two will take the first hansom, Watson and I will follow in the second."

Sherlock Holmes was not very communicative during the long drive, and lay back in the cab humming the tunes which he had heard in the afternoon. We rattled through an endless labyrinth of gas-lit streets until we emerged into Farringdon Street.

"We are close there now," my friend remarked. "This fellow Merryweather is a bank director and personally interested in the matter. I thought it as well to have Jones with us also. He is not a bad fellow, though an absolute imbecile in his profession. He has one positive virtue. He is as brave as a bulldog, and as tenacious as a lobster if he gets his claws upon any one. Here we are, and they are waiting for us."

We had reached the same crowded thoroughfare in which we had found ourselves in the morning. Our cabs were dismissed, and following the guidance of Mr. Merryweather, we passed down a narrow passage, and through a side door which he opened for us. Within there was a small corridor, which ended in a very massive iron gate. This also was opened, and led down a flight of winding stone steps, which terminated at another formidable gate. Mr. Merryweather stopped to light a lantern, and then conducted us down a dark earth-smelling passage, and so, after opening a third door, into a huge vault or cellar, which was piled all round with crates and massive boxes.

"You are not very vulnerable from above," Holmes

remarked, as he held up the lantern and gazed about him.

"Nor from below," said Mr. Merryweather, striking his stick upon the flags which lined the floor. "Why, dear me, it sounds quite hollow!" he remarked, looking up in surprise.

"I must really ask you to be a little more quiet," said Holmes, severely. "You have already imperiled the whole success of our expedition. Might I beg that you would have the goodness to sit down upon one of those boxes, and not to interfere?"

The solemn Mr. Merryweather perched himself upon a crate, with a very injured expression upon his face, while Holmes fell upon his knees upon the floor, and, with the lantern and a magnifying lens, began to examine minutely the cracks between the stones. A few seconds sufficed to satisfy him, for he sprang to his feet again, and put his glass in his pocket.

"We have at least an hour before us," he remarked, "for they can hardly take any steps until the good pawnbroker is safely in bed. Then they will not lose a minute, for the sooner they do their work the longer time they will have for their escape. We are at present, doctor—as no doubt you have divined—in the cellar of the City branch of one of the principal London banks. Mr. Merryweather is the chairman of directors, and he will explain to you that there are reasons why the more daring criminals of London should take a considerable interest in this cellar at present."

"It is our French gold," whispered the director. "We

have had several warnings that an attempt might be
made upon it."

"Your French gold?"

"Yes. We had occasion some months ago to strength-
en our resources, and borrowed, for that purpose, thirty
thousand napoleons from the Bank of France. It has
become known that we have never had occasion to un-
pack the money, and that it is still lying in our cellar.
The crate upon which I sit contains two thousand
napoleons packed between layers of lead foil. Our re-
serve of bullion is much larger at present than is usually
kept in a single branch office, and the directors have
had misgivings upon the subject."

"Which were very well justified," observed Holmes.
"And now it is time that we arranged our little plans.
I expect that within an hour matters will come to a
head. In the meantime, Mr. Merryweather, we must
put the screen over that dark lantern."

"And sit in the dark?"

"I am afraid so. I had brought a pack of cards in my
pocket, and I thought that, as we were a *partie carrée,*
you might have your rubber after all. But I see that
the enemy's preparations have gone so far that we cannot risk the presence of a light. And, first of all, we
must choose our positions. These are daring men, and,
though we shall take them at a disadvantage, they may
do us some harm, unless we are careful. I shall stand
behind this crate, and do you conceal yourself behind
those. Then, when I flash a light upon them, close in
swiftly. If they fire, Watson, have no compunction

about shooting them down."

I placed my revolver, cocked, upon the top of the wooden case behind which I crouched. Holmes shot the slide across the front of his lantern, and left us in pitch darkness—such an absolute darkness as I have never before experienced. The smell of hot metal remained to assure us that the light was still there, ready to flash out at a moment's notice. To me, with my nerves worked up to a pitch of expectancy, there was something depressing and subduing in the sudden gloom, and in the cold, dank air of the vault.

"They have but one retreat," whispered Holmes. "That is back through the house into Saxe-Coburg Square. I hope that you have done what I asked you, Jones?"

"I have an inspector and two officers waiting at the front door."

"Then we have stopped all the holes. And now we must be silent and wait."

What a time it seemed! From comparing notes afterwards, it was but an hour and a quarter, yet it appeared to me that the night must have almost gone, and the dawn be breaking above us. My limbs were weary and stiff, for I feared to change my position, yet my nerves were worked up to the highest pitch of tension, and my hearing was so acute that I could not only hear the gentle breathing of my companions, but I could distinguish the deeper, heavier inbreath of the bulky Jones from the thin, sighing note of the bank director. From my position I could look over the case in the direction of the floor. Suddenly my eyes caught the glint of a light.

At first it was but a lurid spark upon the stone pavement. Then it lengthened out until it became a yellow line, and then, without any warning or sound, a gash seemed to open and a hand appeared, a white, almost womanly hand, which felt about in the center of the little area of light. For a minute or more the hand, with its writhing fingers, protruded out of the floor. Then it was withdrawn as suddenly as it appeared, and all was dark again save the single lurid spark, which marked a chink between the stones.

Its disappearance, however, was but momentary. With a rending, tearing sound, one of the broad white stones turned over upon its side, and left a square, gaping hole, through which streamed the light of a lantern. Over the edge there peeped a clean-cut, boyish face, which looked keenly about it, and then, with a hand on either side of the aperture, drew itself shoulder-high and waist-high, until one knee rested upon the edge. In another instant he stood at the side of the hole, and was hauling after him a companion, lithe and small like himself, with a pale face and a shock of very red hair.

"It's all clear," he whispered. "Have you the chisel and the bags? Great Scott! Jump, Archie, jump, and I'll swing for it!"

Sherlock Holmes had sprung out and seized the intruder by the collar. The other dived down the hole, and I heard the sound of rending cloth as Jones clutched at his skirts. The light flashed upon the barrel of a revolver, but Holmes's hunting crop came down on the man's wrist, and the pistol clinked upon the stone floor.

"It's no use, John Clay," said Holmes, blandly, "you have no chance at all."

"So I see," the other answered, with the utmost coolness. "I fancy that my pal is all right, though I see you have got his coat-tails."

"There are three men waiting for him at the door," said Holmes.

"Oh, indeed. You seem to have done the thing very completely. I must compliment you."

"And I you," Holmes answered. "Your red-headed idea was very new and effective."

"You'll see your pal again presently," said Jones. "He's quicker at climbing down holes than I am. Just hold out while I fix the derbies."

"I beg that you will not touch me with your filthy hands," remarked our prisoner, as the handcuffs clattered upon his wrists. "You may not be aware that I have royal blood in my veins. Have the goodness also, when you address me, always to say 'sir' and 'please.' "

"All right," said Jones, with a stare and a snigger. "Well, would you please, sir, march upstairs where we can get a cab to carry your highness to the police station."

"That is better," said John Clay, serenely. He made a sweeping bow to the three of us, and walked quietly off in the custody of the detective."

"Really, Mr. Holmes," said Mr. Merryweather, as we followed them from the cellar, "I do not know how the bank can thank you or repay you. There is no doubt that you have detected and defeated in the most complete manner one of the most determined attempts at bank robbery that have ever come within my experience."

"I have had one or two little scores of my own to settle with Mr. John Clay," said Holmes. "I have been at some small expense over this matter, which I shall expect the bank to refund, but beyond that I am amply repaid by having had an experience which is in many ways unique, and by hearing the very remarkable narrative of the Red-headed League."

"You see, Watson," he explained, in the early hours of the morning, as we sat over a glass of whiskey and soda in Baker Street, "it was perfectly obvious from the first that the only possible object of this rather fantastic business of the advertisement of the League, and the copying of the 'Encyclopaedia,' must be to get this not over-bright pawnbroker out of the way for a number of hours every day. It was a curious way of managing it, but really it would be difficult to suggest a better. The method was no doubt suggested to Clay's ingenious mind by the color of his accomplice's hair. The four pounds a week was a lure which must draw him, and what was it to them, who were playing for thousands? They put in the advertisement, one rogue has the temporary office, the other rogue incites the man to apply for it, and together they manage to secure his absence every morning in the week. From the time that I heard of the assistant having come for half wages, it was obvious to me that he had some strong motive for securing the situation."

"But how could you guess what the motive was?"

"Had there been women in the house, I should have suspected a mere vulgar intrigue. That, however, was out of the question. The man's business was a small one, and there was nothing in his house which could account for such elaborate preparations, and such an expenditure as they were at. It must then be something out of the house. What could it be? I thought of the assistant's fondness for photography, and his trick of vanishing into the cellar. The cellar! There was the end of this tangled clue. Then I made inquiries as to this mysterious assistant, and found that I had to deal with one of the coolest and most daring criminals in London. He was doing something in the cellar—something which took many hours a day for months on end. What could it be, once more? I could think of nothing save that he was running a tunnel to some other building.

"So far I had got when we went to visit the scene of action. I surprised you by beating upon the pavement with my stick. I was ascertaining whether the cellar stretched out in front or behind. It was not in front. Then I rang the bell, and, as I hoped, the assistant answered it. We have had some skirmishes, but we had never set eyes upon each other before. I hardly looked at his face. His knees were what I wished to see. You must yourself have remarked how worn, wrinkled, and stained they were. They spoke of those hours of burrowing. The only remaining point was what they were burrowing for. I walked round the corner, saw that the City and Suburban Bank abutted on our friend's premises, and felt that I had solved my problem. When you drove home after the concert I called upon Scotland Yard, and upon the chairman of the bank directors, with the result that you have seen."

"And how could you tell that they would make their attempt to-night?" I asked.

"Well, when they closed their League offices that was a sign that they cared no longer about Mr. Jabez Wilson's presence; in other words, that they had completed their tunnel. But it was essential that they should use it soon, as it might be discovered, or the bullion might be removed. Saturday would suit them better than any other day, as it would give them two days for their escape. For all these reasons I expected them to come to-night."

"You reasoned it out beautifully," I exclaimed, in unfeigned admiration. "It is so long a chain, and yet every link rings true."

"It saved me from ennui," he answered, yawning. "Alas! I already feel it closing in upon me. My life is spent in one long effort to escape from the commonplaces of existence. These little problems help me to do so."

"And you are a benefactor of the race," said I. He shrugged his shoulders. "Well, perhaps, after all, it is

of some little use," he remarked. " 'L'homme c'est rien
—l'oeuvre c'est tout,' as Gustave Flaubert wrote to
Georges Sand."

A SCANDAL IN BOHEMIA

TO SHERLOCK HOLMES she is always *the* woman. I have seldom heard him mention her under any other name. In his eyes she eclipses and predominates the whole of her sex. It was not that he felt any emotion akin to love for Irene Adler. All emotions, and that one particularly, were abhorrent to his cold, precise but admirably balanced mind. He was, I take it, the most perfect reasoning and observing machine that the world has seen, but as a lover he would have placed himself in a false position. He never spoke of the softer passions, save with a gibe and a sneer. They were admirable things for the observer—excellent for drawing the veil from men's motives and actions. But for the trained reasoner to admit such intrusions into his own delicate and finely adjusted temperament was to introduce a distracting factor which might throw a doubt upon all his mental results. Grit in a sensitive instrument, or a crack in one of his own high-power lenses, would not be more disturbing than a strong emotion in a nature such as his. And yet there was but one woman to him, and that woman was the late Irene Adler, of dubious and questionable memory.

I had seen little of Holmes lately. My marriage had drifted us away from each other. My own complete happiness, and the home-centered interests which rise up around the man who first finds himself master of his own establishment, were sufficient to absorb all my attention, while Holmes, who loathed every form of society with his whole Bohemian soul, remained in our lodgings in Baker Street, buried among his old books, and alternating from week to week between cocaine and ambition, the drowsiness of the drug, and the fierce energy of his own keen nature. He was still, as ever, deeply attracted by the study of crime, and occupied his immense faculties and extraordinary powers of observation in following out those clues, and clearing up those mysteries which had been abandoned as hopeless by the official police. From time to time I heard some vague account of his doings: of his summons to Odessa in the case of the Trepoff murder, of his clearing up of the singular tragedy of the Atkinson brothers at Trincomalee, and finally of the mission which he had accomplished so delicately and successfully for the reigning family of Holland. Beyond these signs of his activity, however, which I merely shared with all the readers of the daily press, I knew little of my former friend and companion.

One night—it was on the twentieth of March, 1888—I was returning from a journey to a patient (for I had now returned to civil practice), when my way led me through Baker Street. As I passed the well-remembered door, which must always be associated in my mind with my wooing, and with the dark incidents of the *Study in Scarlet,* I was seized with a keen desire to see Holmes again, and to know how he was employing his extraordinary powers. His rooms were brilliantly lit, and, even as I looked up, I saw his tall, spare figure pass twice in a dark silhouette against the blind. He was pacing the room swiftly, eagerly, with his head sunk upon his chest and his hands clasped behind him. To me, who knew his every mood and habit, his attitude and manner told their own story. He was at work again. He had risen out of his drug-created dreams and was hot upon the scent of some new problem. I rang the bell and was shown up to the chamber which had formerly been in part my own.

His manner was not effusive. It seldom was; but he was glad, I think, to see me. With hardly a word spoken, but with a kindly eye, he waved me to an armchair, threw across his case of cigars, and indicated a spirit case and a gasogene in the corner. Then he stood before the fire and looked me over in his singular introspective fashion.

"Wedlock suits you," he remarked. "I think, Watson, that you have put on seven and a half pounds since I saw you."

"Seven!" I answered.

"Indeed, I should have thought a little more. Just a trifle more, I fancy, Watson. And in practice again, I observe. You did not tell me that you intended to go into harness."

"Then, how do you know?"

"I see it, deduce it. How do I know that you have been getting yourself very wet lately, and that you have a most clumsy and careless servant girl?"

"My dear Holmes," said I, "this is too much. You would certainly have been burned, had you lived a few centuries ago. It is true that I had a country walk on Thursday and came home in a dreadful mess, but as I have changed my clothes I can't imagine how you deduce it. As to Mary Jane, she is incorrigible, and my wife has given her notice; but there, again, I fail to see how you work it out."

He chuckled to himself and rubbed his long, nervous hands together.

"It is simplicity itself," he said; "my eyes tell me that on the inside of your left shoe, just where the firelight strikes it, the leather is scored by six almost parallel cuts. Obviously they have been caused by someone who has very carelessly scraped round the edges of the sole in order to remove crusted mud from it. Hence, you see, my double deduction that you had been out in vile weather, and that you had a particularly malignant boot-slitting specimen of the London slavey. As to your practice, if a gentleman walks into my rooms smelling of iodoform, with a black mark of nitrate of silver upon his right forefinger, and a bulge on the right side of his top-hat to show where he has secreted his stethoscope, I must be dull, indeed, if I do not pronounce him to be an active member of the medical profession."

I could not help laughing at the ease with which he explained his process of deduction. "When I hear you give your reasons," I remarked, "the thing always appears to me to be so ridiculously simple that I could easily do it myself, though at each successive instance of your reasoning I am baffled until you explain your process. And yet I believe that my eyes are as good as yours."

"Quite so," he answered, lighting a cigarette, and throwing himself down into an armchair. "You see, but you do not observe. The distinction is clear. For example, you have frequently seen the steps which lead up from the hall to this room."

"Frequently."

"And how often?" Holmes continued, dryly.

"Well, some hundreds of times."

"Then how many are there?"

"How many? I don't know."

"Quite so! You have not observed. And yet you have seen. That is just my point. Now, I know that there are seventeen steps, because I have both seen and observed. By the way, since you are interested in these little problems, and since you are good enough to chronicle one or two of my trifling experiences, you may be interested in this." He threw over a sheet of thick, pink-tinted note-paper which had been lying open upon the table. "It came by the last post," said he. "Read it aloud."

The note was undated, and without either signature or address.

There will call upon you tonight, at a quarter to eight o'clock [it said], a gentleman who desires to consult you upon a matter of the very deepest moment. Your recent services to one of the royal houses of Europe have shown that you are one who may safely be trusted with matters which are of an importance which can hardly be exaggerated. This account of you we have from all quarters received. Be in your chamber then at that hour, and do not take it amiss if your visitor wear a mask.

"This is indeed a mystery," I remarked. "What do you imagine that it means?"

"I have no data yet. It is a capital mistake to theorize before one has data. Insensibly one begins to twist facts to suit theories, instead of theories to suit facts. But the note itself. What do you deduce from it?"

I carefully examined the writing, and the paper upon which it was written.

"The man who wrote it was presumably well to do," I remarked, endeavoring to imitate my companion's processes. "Such paper could not be bought under half a crown a packet. It is peculiarly strong and stiff."

"Peculiar—that is the very word," said Holmes. "It is not an English paper at all. Hold it up to the light."

I did so, and saw a large *"E"* with a small *"g,"* a *"P,"* and a large "*G*" with a small "*t*" woven into the texture of the paper.

"What do you make of that?" asked Holmes.

"The name of the maker, no doubt; or his monogram, rather."

"Not at all. The '*G*' with the small '*t*' stands for 'Gesellschaft,' which is the German for 'Company.' It is a customary contraction like our 'Co.' '*P*,' of course, stands for 'Papier.' Now for the '*Eg.*' Let us glance at our Continental Gazetteer." He took down a heavy brown volume from his shelves. "Eglow, Eglonitz— here we are, Egria. It is in a German-speaking country —in Bohemia, not far from Carlsbad. 'Remarkable as being the scene of the death of Wallenstein, and for its numerous glass-factories and paper-mills.' Ha, ha, my boy, what do you make of that?" His eyes sparkled, and he sent up a great blue triumphant cloud from his cigarette.

"The paper was made in Bohemia," I said.

"Precisely. And the man who wrote the note is a German. Do you note the peculiar construction of the sentence—'This account of you we have from all quarters received.' A Frenchman or Russian could not have written that. It is the German who is so uncourteous to his verbs. It only remains, therefore, to discover what is wanted by this German who writes upon Bohemian paper and prefers wearing a mask to showing his face. And here he comes, if I am not mistaken, to resolve all our doubts."

As he spoke there was the sharp sound of horses'

hoofs and grating wheels against the curb, followed by a sharp pull at the bell. Holmes whistled.

"A pair, by the sound," said he. "Yes," he continued, glancing out of the window. "A nice little brougham and a pair of beauties. A hundred and fifty guineas apiece. There's money in this case, Watson, if there is nothing else."

"I think that I had better go, Holmes."

"Not a bit, Doctor. Stay where you are. I am lost without my Boswell. And this promises to be interesting. It would be a pity to miss it."

"But your client——"

"Never mind him. I may want your help, and so may he. Here he comes. Sit down in that armchair, Doctor, and give us your best attention."

A slow and heavy step, which had been heard upon the stairs and in the passage, paused immediately outside the door. Then there was a loud and authoritative tap.

"Come in!" said Holmes.

A man entered who could hardly have been less than six feet six inches in height, with the chest and limbs of a Hercules. His dress was rich with a richness which would, in England, be looked upon as akin to bad taste. Heavy bands of astrakhan were slashed across the sleeves and fronts of his double-breasted coat, while the deep blue cloak which was thrown over his shoulders was lined with flame-colored silk and secured at the neck with a brooch which consisted of a single flaming beryl. Boots which extended halfway up his calves, and which were trimmed at the tops with rich brown fur, completed the impression of barbaric opulence which was suggested by his whole appearance. He carried a broad-brimmed hat in his hand, while he wore across the upper part of his face, extending down past the cheekbones, a black vizard mask, which he had apparently adjusted that very moment, for his hand was still raised to it as he entered. From the lower part of the face he appeared to be a man of strong character, with a thick, hanging lip, and a long, straight chin suggestive of resolution pushed to the length of obstinacy.

"You had my note?" he asked with a deep harsh voice and a strong marked German accent. "I told you that I would call." He looked from one to the other of us, as if uncertain which to address.

"Pray take a seat," said Holmes. "This is my friend and colleague, Dr. Watson, who is occasionally good enough to help me in my cases. Whom have I the honor to address?"

"You may address me as the Count Von Kramm, a Bohemian nobleman. I understand that this gentleman, your friend, is a man of honor and discretion, whom I may trust with a matter of the most extreme importance. If not, I should much prefer to communicate with you alone."

I rose to go, but Holmes caught me by the wrist and pushed me back into my chair. "It is both, or none," said he. "You may say before this gentleman anything which you may say to me."

The Count shrugged his broad shoulders. "Then I must begin," said he, "by binding you both to absolute secrecy for two years; at the end of that time the matter will be of no importance. At present it is not too much to say that it is of such weight it may have an influence upon European history."

"I promise," said Holmes.

"And I."

"You will excuse this mask," continued our strange visitor. "The august person who employs me wishes his agent to be unknown to you, and I may confess at once that the title by which I have just called myself is not exactly my own."

"I was aware of it," said Holmes drily.

"The circumstances are of great delicacy, and every precaution has to be taken to quench what might grow to be an immense scandal and seriously compromise one of the reigning families of Europe. To speak plainly, the matter implicates the great House of Ormstein, hereditary kings of Bohemia."

"I was also aware of that," murmured Holmes, settling himself down in his armchair and closing his eyes.

Our visitor glanced with some apparent surprise at the languid, lounging figure of the man who had been no doubt depicted to him as the most incisive reasoner and most energetic agent in Europe. Holmes slowly reopened his eyes and looked impatiently at his gigantic client.

"If your Majesty would condescend to state your case," he remarked as he eyed his visitor steadily. "I should be better able to advise you."

· The man sprang from his chair and paced up and down the room in uncontrollable agitation. Then, with a gesture of desperation, he tore the mask from his face and hurled it upon the ground. "You are right," he cried; "I am the King. Why should I attempt to conceal it?"

"Why, indeed?" murmured Holmes. "Your Majesty had not spoken before I was aware that I was addressing Wilhelm Gottsreich Sigismond von Ormstein, Grand Duke of Cassel-Felstein, and hereditary King of Bohemia."

"But you can understand," said our strange visitor, sitting down once more and passing his hand over his high white forehead, "you can understand that I am not accustomed to doing such business in my own person. Yet the matter was so delicate that I could not confide it to an agent without putting myself in his power. I have come incognito from Prague for the purpose of consulting you."

"Then, pray consult," said Holmes, shutting his eyes once more.

"The facts are briefly these: Some five years ago, during a lengthy visit to Warsaw, I made the acquaintance of the well-known adventuress, Irene Adler. The name is no doubt familiar to you."

"Kindly look her up in my index, Doctor," murmured Holmes without opening his eyes. For many years he had adopted a system of docketing all paragraphs concerning men and things, so that it was difficult to name a subject or a person on which he could not at once furnish information. In this case I found her biography sandwiched in between that of a Hebrew rabbi and that of a staff-commander who had written a monograph upon the deep-sea fishes.

"Let me see!" said Holmes. "Hum! Born in New Jersey in the year 1858. Contralto—hum! La Scala, hum! Prima donna Imperial Opera of Warsaw—Yes! Retired from operatic stage—ha! Living in London—quite so! Your Majesty, as I understand, became entangled with this young person, wrote her some compromising letters, and is now desirous of getting those letters back."

"Precisely so. But how——"

"Was there a secret marriage?"

"None."

"No legal papers or certificates?"

"None."

"Then I fail to follow your Majesty. If this young person should produce her letters for blackmailing or other purposes, how is she to prove their authenticity?"

"There is the writing."

"Pooh, pooh! Forgery."

"My private note-paper."

"Stolen."

"My own seal."

"Imitated."

"My photograph."

"Bought."

"We were both in the photograph."

"Oh, dear! That is very bad! Your Majesty has indeed committed an indiscretion."

"I was mad—insane."

"You have compromised yourself seriously."

"I was only Crown Prince then. I was young. I am but thirty now."

"It must be recovered."

"We have tried and failed."

"Your Majesty must pay. It must be bought."

"She will not sell."

"Stolen, then."

"Five attempts have been made. Twice burglars in my pay ransacked her house. Once we diverted her luggage when she travelled. Twice she has been waylaid. There has been no result."

"No sign of it?"

"Absolutely none."

Holmes laughed. "It is quite a pretty little problem," said he.

"But a very serious one to me," returned the King reproachfully.

"Very, indeed. And what does she propose to do with the photograph?"

"To ruin me."

"But how?"

"I am about to be married."

"So I have heard."

"To Clotilde Lothman von Saxe-Meningen, second daughter of the King of Scandinavia. You may know the strict principles of her family. She is herself the very soul of delicacy. A shadow of a doubt as to my conduct would bring the matter to an end."

"And Irene Adler?" Holmes said, a trifle sharply.

"Threatens to send them the photograph. And she will do it. I know that she will do it. You do not know her, but she has a soul of steel. She has the face of the most beautiful of women, and the mind of the most resolute of men. Rather than I should marry another woman, there are no lengths to which she would not go—none."

"You are sure that she has not sent it yet?"

"I am sure."

"And why?"

"Because she has said that she would send it on the day when the betrothal was publicly proclaimed. That will be next Monday."

"Oh, then we have three days yet," said Holmes with a yawn. "That is very fortunate, as I have one or two matters of importance to look into just at present. Your Majesty will, of course, stay in London for the present?"

"Certainly. You will find me at the Langham under the name of the Count Von Kramm."

"Then I shall drop you a line to let you know how we progress."

"Pray do so. I shall be all anxiety."

"Then, as to money?"

"You have carte blanche."

"Absolutely?"

"I tell you that I would give one of the provinces of my kingdom to have that photograph."

"And," said Holmes, "for the present expenses?"

The King took a heavy chamois leather bag from under his cloak and laid it on the table.

"There are three hundred pounds in gold and seven hundred in notes," he said.

Holmes scribbled a receipt upon a sheet of his note-book and handed it to him.

"And Mademoiselle's address?" he asked.

"Is Briony Lodge, Serpentine Avenue, St. John's Wood."

Holmes took a note of it. "One other question," said he. "Was the photograph a cabinet?"

"It was."

"Then, good-night, your Majesty, and I trust that we shall soon have some good news for you. And good-night, Watson," he added, as the wheels of the royal brougham rolled down the street. "If you will be good enough to call tomorrow afternoon at three o'clock I should like to chat this little matter over with you."

II

At three o'clock precisely I was at Baker Street, but Holmes had not yet returned. The landlady informed me that he had left the house shortly after eight o'clock in the morning. I sat down beside the fire, however, with the intention of awaiting him, however long he might be. I was already deeply interested in his inquiry, for, though it was surrounded by none of the grim and strange features which were associated with the two crimes which I have already recorded, still, the nature of the case and the exalted station of his client gave it a character of its own. Indeed, apart from the nature of the investigation which my friend had on hand, there was something in his masterly grasp of a situation, and his keen, incisive reasoning, which made it a pleasure to me to study his system of work, and to follow the quick, subtle methods by which he disentangled the most inextricable mysteries. So accustomed was I to his invariable success that the very possibility of his failing had ceased to enter into my head.

It was close upon four before the door opened, and a drunken-looking groom, ill-kempt and side-whiskered, with an inflamed face and disreputable clothes, walked into the room. Accustomed as I was to my friend's amazing powers in the use of disguises, I had to look three times before I was certain that it was indeed he. With a nod he vanished into the bedroom, whence he emerged in five minutes tweed-suited and respectable, as of old. Putting his hands into his pockets, he stretched out his legs in front of the fire and laughed heartily for some minutes.

"Well, really!" he cried, and then he choked and laughed again until he was obliged to lie back, limp and helpless, in the chair.

"What is it?" I asked, thoroughly bewildered.

"It's quite too funny. I am sure you could never guess how I employed my morning, or what I ended by doing."

"I can't imagine. I suppose that you have been watching the habits, and perhaps the house, of Miss Irene Adler."

"Quite so; but the sequel was rather unusual. I will tell you, however. I left the house a little after eight o'clock this morning in the character of a groom out of work. There is a wonderful sympathy and freemasonry among horsy men. Be one of them, and you will know all that there is to know. I soon found Briony Lodge. It is a *bijou* villa, with a garden at the back, but built out in front right up to the road, two stories. Chubb lock to the door. Large sitting-room on the right side, well furnished, with long windows almost to the floor, and those preposterous English window fasteners which a child could open. Behind there was nothing remarkable, save that the passage window could be reached from the top of the coach-house. I walked round it and examined it closely from every point of view, but without noting anything else of interest.

"I then lounged down the street and found, as I expected, that there was a mews in a lane which runs down by one wall of the garden. I lent the ostlers a hand in rubbing down their horses, and received in exchange twopence, a glass of half and half, two fills of shag tobacco, and as much information as I could desire about Miss Adler, to say nothing of half a dozen other people in the neighborhood in whom I was not in the least interested, but whose biographies I was compelled to listen to."

"And what of Irene Adler?" I asked.

"Oh, she has turned all the men's heads down in that part. She is the daintiest thing under a bonnet on this planet. So say the Serpentine-mews, to a man. She lives quietly, sings at concerts, drives out at five every day, and returns at seven sharp for dinner. Seldom goes out at other times, except when she sings. Has only one male visitor, but a good deal of him. He is dark, handsome, and dashing, never calls less than once a day, and often twice. He is a Mr. Godfrey Norton, of the Inner Temple. See the advantages of a cabman as a confidant. They had driven him home a dozen times from Serpentine-mews, and knew all about him. When I had listened to all they had to tell, I began to walk up and down near Briony Lodge once more, and to think over my plan of campaign.

"This Godfrey Norton was evidently an important factor in the matter. He was a lawyer. That sounded ominous. What was the relation between them, and what the object of his repeated visits? Was she his client, his friend, or his mistress? If the former, she had probably transferred the photograph to his keeping. If the latter, it was less likely. On the issue of this question depended whether I should continue my work at Briony Lodge, or turn my attention to the gentleman's chambers in the Temple. It was a delicate point, and it widened the field of my inquiry. I fear that I bore you with these details, but I have to let you see my little difficulties, if you are to understand the situation."

"I am following you closely," I answered.

"I was still balancing the matter in my mind when a

hansom cab drove up to Briony Lodge, and a gentleman sprang out. He was a remarkably handsome man, dark, aquiline, and moustached—evidently the man of whom I had heard. He appeared to be in a great hurry, shouted to the cabman to wait, and brushed past the maid who opened the door with the air of a man who was thoroughly at home.

"He was in the house about half an hour, and I could catch glimpses of him in the windows of the sitting-room, pacing up and down, talking excitedly, and waving his arms. Of her I could see nothing. Presently he emerged, looking even more flurried than before. As he stepped up to the cab, he pulled a gold watch from his pocket and looked at it earnestly, 'Drive like the devil,' he shouted, 'first to Gross & Hankey's in Regent Street, and then to the Church of St. Monica in the Edgware Road. Half a guinea if you do it in twenty minutes!'

"Away they went, and I was just wondering whether I should not do well to follow them when up the lane came a neat little landau, the coachman with his coat only half-buttoned, and his tie under his ear, while all the tags of his harness were sticking out of the buckles. It hadn't pulled up before she shot out of the hall door and into it. I only caught a glimpse of her at the moment, but she was a lovely woman, with a face that a man might die for.

" 'The Church of St. Monica, John,' she cried, 'and half a sovereign if you reach it in twenty minutes.'

"This was quite too good to lose, Watson. I was just

balancing whether I should run for it, or whether I should perch behind her landau, when a cab came through the street. The driver looked twice at such a shabby fare, but I jumped in before he could object. 'The Church of St. Monica,' said I, 'and half a sovereign if you reach it in twenty minutes.' It was twenty-five minutes to twelve, and of course it was clear enough what was in the wind.

"My cabby drove fast. I don't think I ever drove faster, but the others were there before us. The cab and the landau with their steaming horses were in front of the door when I arrived. I paid the man and hurried into the church. There was not a soul there save the two whom I had followed and a surpliced clergyman, who seemed to be expostulating with them. They were all three standing in a knot in front of the altar. I lounged up the side aisle like any other idler who has dropped into a church. Suddenly, to my surprise, the three at the altar faced round to me, and Godfrey Norton came running as hard as he could towards me.

" 'Thank God!' he cried. 'You'll do. Come! Come!'

" 'What then?' I asked.

" 'Come, man, come, only three minutes, or it won't be legal.'

"I was half-dragged up to the altar, and before I knew where I was I found myself mumbling responses which were whispered in my ear, and vouching for things of which I knew nothing, and generally assisting in the secure tying up of Irene Adler, spinster, to Godfrey Norton, bachelor. It was all done in an instant, and there was the gentleman thanking me on the one side and the lady on the other, while the clergyman beamed on me in front. It was the most preposterous position in which I ever found myself in my life, and it was the thought of it that started me laughing just now. It seems that there had been some informality about their license, that the clergyman absolutely refused to marry them without a witness of some sort, and that my lucky appearance saved the bridegroom from having to sally out into the streets in search of a best man. The bride gave me a sovereign, and I mean to wear it on my watch-chain in memory of the occasion."

"This is a very unexpected turn of affairs," said I; "and what then?"

"Well, I found my plans very seriously menaced. It looked as if the pair might take an immediate departure, and so necessitate very prompt and energetic measures on my part. At the church door, however, they separated, he driving back to the Temple, and she to her own house. 'I shall drive out in the park at five as usual,' she said as she left him. I heard no more. They drove away in different directions, and I went off to make my own arrangements."

"Which are?"

"Some cold beef and a glass of beer," he answered, ringing the bell. "I have been too busy to think of food, and I am likely to be busier still this evening. By the way, Doctor, I shall want your coöperation."

"I shall be delighted."

"You don't mind breaking the law?"

"Not in the least."

"Nor running a chance of arrest?"

"Not in a good cause."

"Oh, the cause is excellent!"

"Then I am your man."

"I was sure that I might rely on you."

"But what is it you wish?"

"When Mrs. Turner has brought in the tray I will make it clear to you. Now," he said as he turned hungrily on the simple fare that our landlady had provided, "I must discuss it while I eat, for I have not much time. It is nearly five now. In two hours we must be on the scene of action. Miss Irene, or Madame, rather, returns from her drive at seven. We must be at Briony Lodge to meet her."

"And what then?"

"You must leave that to me. I have already arranged what is to occur. There is only one point on which I must insist. You must not interfere, come what may. You understand?"

"I am to be neutral?"

"To do nothing whatever. There will probably be some small unpleasantness. Do not join in it. It will end in my being conveyed into the house. Four or five minutes afterwards the sitting-room window will open. You are to station yourself close to that open window."

"Yes."

"You are to watch me, for I will be visible to you."

"Yes."

"And when I raise my hand—so—you will throw into the room what I give you to throw, and will, at the same time, raise the cry of fire. You quite follow me?"

"Entirely."

"It is nothing very formidable," he said, taking a long cigar-shaped roll from his pocket. "It is an ordinary plumber's smoke-rocket, fitted with a cap at either end to make it self-lighting. Your task is confined to that. When you raise your cry of fire, it will be taken up by quite a number of people. You may then walk to the end of the street, and I will rejoin you in ten minutes. I hope that I have made myself clear?"

"I am to remain neutral, to get near the window, to watch you, and at the signal to throw in this object, then to raise the cry of fire, and to wait you at the corner of the street."

"Precisely."

"Then you may entirely rely on me."

"That is excellent. I think, perhaps, it is almost time that I prepare for the new rôle I have to play."

He disappeared into his bedroom and returned in a few minutes in the character of an amiable and simple-minded Nonconformist clergyman. His broad black hat, his baggy trousers, his white tie, his sympathetic smile, and general look of peering and benevolent curiosity were such as Mr. John Hare alone could have equalled. It was not merely that Holmes changed his costume. His expression, his manner, his very soul seemed to vary with every fresh part that he assumed. The stage lost a fine actor, even as science lost an acute reasoner, when he became a specialist in crime.

It was a quarter past six when we left Baker Street, and it still wanted ten minutes to the hour when we found ourselves in Serpentine Avenue. It was already dusk, and the lamps were just being lighted as we paced up and down in front of Briony Lodge, waiting for the coming of its occupant. The house was just such as I had pictured it from Sherlock Holmes's succinct description, but the locality appeared to be less private than I expected. On the contrary, for a small street in a quiet neighborhood, it was remarkably animated. There was a group of shabbily dressed men smoking and laughing in a corner, a scissors-grinder with his wheel, two guardsmen who were flirting with a nurse-girl, and several well-dressed young men who were lounging up and down with cigars in their mouths.

"You see," remarked Holmes, as we paced to and fro in front of the house, "this marriage rather simplifies matters. The photograph becomes a double-edged weapon now. The chances are that she would be as averse to its being seen by Mr. Godfrey Norton, as our client is to its coming to the eyes of his princess. Now the question is, Where are we to find the photograph?"

"Where, indeed?"

"It is most unlikely that she carries it about with her. It is cabinet size. Too large for easy concealment about a woman's dress. She knows that the King is capable of having her waylaid and searched. Two attempts of the sort have already been made. We may take it, then, that she does not carry it about with her."

"Where, then?" I was at another lost.

"Her banker or her lawyer. There is that double possibility. But I am inclined to think neither. Women are naturally secretive, and they like to do their own secreting. Why should she hand it over to anyone else? She could trust her own guardianship, but she could not tell what indirect or political influence might be brought to bear upon a business man. Besides, remember that she had resolved to use it within a few days. It must be where she can lay her hands upon it. It must be in her own house."

"But it has twice been burgled."

"Pshaw! They did not know how to look."

"But how will you look?"

"I will not look."

"What then?"

"I will get her to show me."

"But she will refuse."

"She will not be able to. But I hear the rumble of wheels. It is her carriage. Now carry out my orders to the letter."

As he spoke the gleam of the side-lights of a carriage came round the curve of the avenue. It was a smart little landau which rattled up to the door of Briony Lodge. As it pulled up, one of the loafing men at the corner dashed forward to open the door in the hope of earning a copper, but was elbowed away by another loafer, who had rushed up with the same intention. A fierce quarrel broke out, which was increased by the two guardsmen, who took sides with one of the

loungers, and by the scissors-grinder, who was equally
hot upon the other side. A blow was struck, and in an
instant the lady, who had stepped from her carriage,
was the centre of a little knot of flushed and struggling
men, who struck savagely at each other with their fists
and sticks. Holmes dashed into the crowd to protect the
lady; but just as he reached her he gave a cry and
dropped to the ground, with the blood running freely
down his face. At his fall the guardsmen took to their
heels in one direction and the loungers in the other,
while a number of better-dressed people, who had
watched the scuffle without taking part in it, crowded
in to help the lady and to attend to the injured man.
Irene Adler, as I will still call her, had hurried up the
steps; but she stood at the top with her superb figure
outlined against the lights of the hall, looking back
into the street.

"Is the poor gentleman much hurt?" she asked.

"He is dead," cried several voices.

"No, no, there's life in him!" shouted another. "But
he'll be gone before you can get him to hospital."

"He's a brave fellow," said a woman. "They would
have had the lady's purse and watch if it hadn't been
for him. They were a gang, and a rough one, too. Ah,
he's breathing now."

"He can't lie in the street. May we bring him in,
marm?"

"Surely. Bring him into the sitting-room. There is a
comfortable sofa. This way, please!"

Slowly and solemnly he was borne into Briony

Lodge and laid out in the principal room, while I still observed the proceedings from my post by the window. The lamps had been lit, but the blinds had not been drawn, so that I could see Holmes as he lay upon the couch. I do not know whether he was seized with compunction at that moment for the part he was playing, but I know that I never felt more heartily ashamed of myself in my life than when I saw the beautiful creature against whom I was conspiring, or the grace and kindliness with which she waited upon the injured man. And yet it would be the blackest treachery to Holmes to draw back now from the part which he had intrusted to me. I hardened my heart, and took the smoke-rocket from under my ulster. After all, I thought, we are not injuring her. We are but preventing her from injuring another.

Holmes had sat up upon the couch, and I saw him motion like a man who is in need of air. A maid rushed across and threw open the window. At the same instant I saw him raise his hand, and at the signal I tossed my rocket into the room with a cry of "Fire!" The word was no sooner out of my mouth than the whole crowd of spectators, well dressed and ill—gentlemen, ostlers, and servant-maids—joined in a general shriek of "Fire!" Thick clouds of smoke curled through the room and out at the open window. I caught a glimpse of rushing figures, and a moment later the voice of Holmes from within assuring them that it was a false alarm. Slipping through the shouting crowd I made my way to the corner of the street, and in ten minutes was rejoiced to find my friend's arm in mine, and to get away from the scene of uproar. He walked swiftly and in silence for some few minutes until we had turned down one of the quiet streets which lead towards the Edgware Road.

"You did it very nicely, Doctor," he remarked. "Nothing could have been better. It is all right."

"You have the photograph?"

"I know where it is."

"And how did you find out?"

"She showed me, as I told you she would."

"I am still in the dark."

"I do not wish to make a mystery," said he, laughing. "The matter was perfectly simple. You, of course, saw that everyone in the street was an accomplice. They were all engaged for the evening."

"I guessed as much."

"Then, when the row broke out, I had a little moist red paint in the palm of my hand. I rushed forward, fell down, clapped my hand to my face, and became a piteous spectacle. It is an old trick."

"That also I could fathom."

"Then they carried me in. She was bound to have me in. What else could she do? And into her sitting-room, which was the very room which I suspected. It lay between that and her bedroom, and I was determined to see which. They laid me on a couch, I motioned for air, they were compelled to open the window, and you had your chance."

"How did that help you?"

"It was all-important. When a woman thinks that her house is on fire, her instinct is at once to rush to the thing which she values most. It is a perfectly overpowering impulse, and I have more than once taken advantage of it. In the case of the Darlington substitution scandal it was of use to me, and also in the Arnsworth Castle business. A married woman grabs at her baby; an unmarried one reaches for her jewel-box. Now it was clear to me that our lady of today had nothing in the house more precious to her than what we are in quest of. She would rush to secure it. The alarm of fire was admirably done. The smoke and shouting were enough to shake nerves of steel. She responded beautifully. The photograph is in a recess behind a sliding panel just above the right bell-pull. She was there in an instant, and I caught a glimpse of it as she half-drew it out. When I cried out that it was a false alarm, she replaced it, glanced at the rocket, rushed from the room, and I have not seen her since. I rose, and, making my excuses, escaped from the house. I hesitated whether to attempt to secure the photograph at once; but the coachman had come in, and as he was watching me narrowly it seemed safer to wait. A little over-precipitance may ruin all."

"And now?" I asked.

"Our quest is practically finished. I shall call with the King tomorrow, and with you, if you care to come with us. We will be shown into the sitting-room to wait for the lady, but it is probable that when she comes she may find neither us nor the photograph. It might be a satisfaction to his Majesty to regain it with his own hands."

"And when will you call?"

"At eight in the morning. She will not be up, so that we shall have a clear field. Besides, we must be prompt, for this marriage may mean a complete change in her life and habits. I must wire to the King without delay."

We had reached Baker Street and had stopped at the door. He was searching his pockets for the key when someone passing said:

"Good-night, Mister Sherlock Holmes."

There were several people on the pavement at the time, but the greeting appeared to come from a slim youth in an ulster who had hurried by.

"I've heard that voice before," said Holmes, staring down the dimly lit street. "Now, I wonder who the deuce that could have been."

III

I slept at Baker Street that night, and we were engaged upon our toast and coffee in the morning when the King of Bohemia rushed into the room.

"You have really got it!" he cried, grasping Sherlock Holmes by either shoulder and looking eagerly into his face.

"Not yet," Holmes said, seeming not at all perturbed.

"But you have hopes?"

"I have hopes."

"Then, come. I am all impatience to be gone."

"We must have a cab."

"No, my brougham is waiting."

"Then that will simplify matters." We descended and started off once more for Briony Lodge.

"Irene Adler is married," remarked Holmes.

"Married! When?"

"Yesterday."

"But to whom?"

"To an English lawyer named Norton."

"But she could not love him."

"I am in hopes that she does."

"And why in hopes?"

"Because it would spare your Majesty all fear of future annoyance. If the lady loves her husband, she does not love your Majesty. If she does not love your Majesty, there is no reason why she should interfere with your Majesty's plan."

"It is true. And yet— Well! I wish she had been of my own station! What a queen she would have made!" He relapsed into a moody silence, which was not broken until we drew up in Serpentine Avenue.

The door of Briony Lodge was open, and an elderly woman stood upon the steps. She watched us with a sardonic eye as we stepped from the brougham.

"Mr. Sherlock Holmes, I believe?" said she.

"I am Mr. Holmes," answered my companion, looking at her with a questioning and rather startled gaze.

"Indeed! My mistress told me that you were likely to call. She left this morning with her husband by the 5:15 train from Charing Cross for the Continent."

"What!" Sherlock Holmes staggered back, white with chagrin and surprise. "Do you mean that she has left England?"

"Never to return."

"And the papers?" asked the King hoarsely. "All is lost."

"We shall see." He pushed past the servant and rushed into the drawing-room, followed by the King and myself. The furniture was scattered about in every direction, with dismantled shelves and open drawers, as if the lady had hurriedly ransacked them before her flight. Holmes rushed at the bell-pull, tore back a small sliding shutter, and, plunging in his hand, pulled out a photograph and a letter. The photograph was of Irene Adler herself in evening dress, the letter was superscribed to "Sherlock Holmes, Esq. To be left till called for." My friend tore it open, and we all three read it together. It was dated at midnight of the preceding night and ran in this way:

My dear Mr. Sherlock Holmes:

You really did it very well. You took me in completely. Until after the alarm of fire, I had not a suspicion. But then, when I found how I had betrayed myself, I began to think. I had been warned against you months ago. I had been told that if the King employed an agent it would certainly be you. And your address had been given me. Yet, with all this, you made me reveal what you wanted to know. Even after I became suspicious, I found it hard to think evil of such a dear, kind old clergyman. But, you know, I have been trained as an actress myself. Male costume is nothing new to me. I often take advantage of the freedom which it gives. I sent

John, the coachman, to watch you, ran upstairs, got into my walking-clothes, as I call them, and came down just as you departed.

Well, I followed you to your door, and so made sure that I was really an object of interest to the celebrated Mr. Sherlock Holmes. Then I, rather imprudently, wished you goodnight, and started for the Temple to see my husband.

We both thought the best resource was flight, when pursued by so formidable an antagonist; so you will find the nest empty when you call tomorrow. As to the photograph, your client may rest in peace. I love and am loved by a better man than he. The King may do what he will without hindrance from one whom he has cruelly wronged. I keep it only to safeguard myself, and to preserve a weapon which will always secure me from any steps which he might take in the future. I leave a photograph which he might care to possess; and I remain, dear Mr. Sherlock Holmes,

> Very truly yours,
> IRENE NORTON, *née* ADLER.

"What a woman—oh, what a woman!" cried the King of Bohemia, when we had all three read this epistle. "Did I not tell you how quick and resolute she was? Would she not have made an admirable queen? Is it not a pity that she was not on my level?"

"From what I have seen of the lady she seems indeed to be on a very different level to your Majesty," said Holmes coldly. "I am sorry that I have not been able to bring your Majesty's business to a more successful conclusion."

"On the contrary, my dear sir," cried the King; "nothing could be more successful. I know that her word is inviolate. The photograph is now as safe as if it were in the fire."

"I am glad to hear your Majesty say so."

"I am immensely indebted to you. Pray tell me in what way I can reward you. This ring—" He slipped an emerald snake ring from his finger and held it out upon the palm of his hand.

"Your Majesty has something which I should value even more highly," said Holmes.

"You have but to name it."

"This photograph!"

The King stared at him in amazement.

"Irene's photograph!" he cried. "Certainly, if you wish it."

"I thank your Majesty. Then there is no more to be done in the matter. I have the honor to wish you a very good-morning." He bowed, and, turning away without observing the hand which the King had stretched out to him, he set off in my company for his chambers.

And that was how a great scandal threatened to affect the kingdom of Bohemia, and how the best plans of Mr. Sherlock Holmes were beaten by a woman's wit. He used to make merry over the cleverness of women, but I have not heard him do it of late. And when he speaks of Irene Adler, or when he refers to her photograph, it is always under the honorable title of *the* woman.